Rescuing Rebecca

Greta Gorham

Published by Trellis Publishing, 2021.

This is a work of fiction. Similarities to real people, places, or events are entirely coincidental.

RESCUING REBECCA

First edition. July 5, 2021.

Copyright © 2021 Greta Gorham.

ISBN: 979-8224592210

Written by Greta Gorham.

RESCUING REBECCA

GRETA GORHAM

It had not been that long ago that Rebecca had wondered why Sara wanted to hear the same bedtime stories again and again. Her daughter, so bright and vibrant and imaginative, surely needed more stimulation than the endless repetition of tales she already knew the end to. But, for all the ways Sara was unpredictable and unique in day to day life, frustrating her teachers and marvelling the elders, in this her daughter was as set in her ways as the frailest grandmother. Rebecca had tried to pretend the fable about the hare and the tortoise didn't bore her, tried to infuse every nightly telling with the same excitement, but at a certain point she had to admit she dreaded them. Once she managed to convince Hans to do it, but Sara swiftly sent her father out of the room. It just wasn't the same, and the same was what she wanted.

But, Rebecca supposed, circumstances could change anything, make the fondest things sour and the dullest things sweet. And now, a year after Hans' accident, a year since widowhood turned every sight that brought back every youthful memory ugly, Rebecca found that insipid fable had become, absurdly, something to hold on to.

Maybe in this was Sara was wise, she thought, as her daughter wriggled below the blankets and Rebecca adjusted them before blowing out the candle. The young seemed to adore unpredictability and once Rebecca had too. She had been considered wild and impetuous, warned again and again that she would never find a husband. She bored easily. Yet when your world was turned upside down and nothing remained where you left it, returning to the recognisable was really not so bad. In that way, Sara had proved herself so much cleverer than her parents ever were. In the days, play and exploration and adventure, a new thing to discover around every corner. By night, the warmth of home and the knowledge that the tortoise would always beat that smug hare. Boredom became comfort and comfort was best shared when you both lost something.

Placing the book on Sara's bedside table (she wondered why she even bothered with it anymore; she knew the words by heart) Rebecca walked out into the hall of her modest house and turned the corner into the kitchen. Flames crackled in the fireplace and the warm smell of dinner still lingered as candles bathed everything in a gentle orange light. Rebecca took it all in and, as she did every night, searched for that old feeling of contentedness at the beautiful home that was hers.

That was a routine she would sooner give up.

She sat at the table and closed her eyes. Another day in which she had done nothing, and she could not understand how nothing could leave her so very tired. Her bones ached and her head throbbed, as if she had spent hours behind a plough when in fact she had spent hours wandering these halls, occasionally checking the windows to see if Sara had returned and avoiding the room where her mother rested and read and waited for Rebecca to walk in so she could sit her down and insist that it was time to find another man.

In a way she resented both Hans and herself. She never saw herself as the kind of woman to need a man to make her feel complete. It took Hans dying to reveal to herself exactly how weak she was without the man she had grown with. As a child had she not insisted that men were stupid and pointless, that she could fare far better alone? That insistence had lasted up until the day Hans first smiled at her, and even sometime after that, albeit in a more half-hearted manner. Now he was gone and Rebecca despised the fact that she could not just seem to get up and pick up where she left off. Even the thought of that made her feel sick.

'Rebecca?'

She glanced up. Her mother, Elsa, stood in the doorway, hand steadying herself on the frame, narrowed eyes still sharp even as the rest of her looked about ready to crumble at any second.

'You should be resting,' Rebecca said with no conviction.

'And you should be leaving this house, and instead you rest. It seems neither of us know what is healthy.' Letting go of the door, Elsa hobbled towards the table. Rebecca rose slightly, ready to guide her, but the old woman shooed her away as she lowered herself into her favourite chair.

'It's late, mother,' Rebecca said.

Elsa snorted. 'And when did you start telling me when my bedtime was? I daresay the grave is a long way off for me yet. Until I'm crawling about like a child, I can still do as I please.'

'You may not be crawling like a child but that attitude is reminiscent of one,' Rebecca muttered.

Elsa raised an eyebrow. 'Oh look, a glimmer of humour. I should alert the elders.'

'I wish your illness had robbed you of your humour.'

'Well that's a cruel wish,' Elsa said. 'Humour might be the only reason I'm still here. And don't make some sarcastic comment thanking my humour. It's beneath you.'

'I would say no such thing,' Rebecca said, despite having been about to say exactly such a thing.

'You should count yourself as lucky that I'm still here,' Elsa said.

Rebecca exhaled. That tiredness was going nowhere. She smiled at her mother. 'Of course I do,' she said softly. 'I thank God for it every day. If you had gone as well I...' She shook her head. 'I know you worry about me mother. But you forget I'm a grown woman. When the time is right I will make myself a part of this community again. I promise. But you have to let me make that decision in my own time.'

'Everyone makes their decisions in their own time,' Elsa said. 'But we are not supposed to exist in a lonely vacuum. Sometimes we need family to give us a little push, however much we may hate them for it.' She smiled and rested a hand on Rebecca's face. 'Much as I am loathe to admit it, you are right. I need to sleep. As do you. Goodnight Rebecca.'

Rebecca didn't stand as her mother pushed herself to her feet and shuffled back towards her room. Her inclination was always to help, but Elsa was too strong willed to allow that, and Rebecca feared there was enough strength left in her to administer a swift kick to anyone who tried.

Alone again, she closed her eyes. She thanked God, as she did every night, that her mother had survived her illness, that she still had a daughter, that she still had her own health. Then she reminded herself that that health may not last if she didn't get some sleep. Her mother was right about that, at least.

But she didn't move. She just sat there until the candles were stubs and the first glimmers of morning light came through the window.

She maintained her smile until Sara had run out the door the next morning, on her way to school. She wondered if the other mothers whispered about the fact that she did not accompany her daughter on the way, but the fact was the school was not that far and frankly the prospect of facing either their false cheeriness or unconcealed pity filled her with dread. Part of her wondered if she would punch one of them, part of her if she would break down and cry then and there. And how would they react to either? More pity, or perhaps growing whispers that it had been a year, that it was time for her to move on. If those whispers had not grown already.

She shook that off. Gossip didn't concern her, not really. Not as much as the changed attitudes of all her friends, who at first had visited her every day when all she wanted was to be alone then less and less when she started to need people around her again. And when she did see them, it was always with that slight tightness in their voice, the widening of their eyes on every word that might be hard for her to hear. In the end it became easier to have nothing to do with any of them because the perpetual reminders of her pain weren't doing anything to help it go away. And that avoidance meant that leaving the house became a fraught, difficult experience no longer worth the trouble.

That was not to say she didn't leave occasionally. It was just a matter of timing. Finding the places where nobody would be during the hours when everyone was occupied; whether at work or tending their children or at school. During those times she would head for the stillness of the forest and enjoy herself away from Elsa's prying and the responsibility to be strong for Sara. She could just... be. And after the year she had had, that was a precious thing indeed.

Today, she decided, was a day for that. An hour of fitful sleep had not done much for her weariness, but in the forest at least she could be tired in daylight, surrounded by the beautiful green and smell of nature. And with Sara having disappeared down the path and Elsa still in bed, there was no better time than now.

So she set out, avoiding the path and heading left across the grass. It was a sunny day, the skies were clearer than they had been in a while and she could smell the warm, familiar, distant scent of the harvest. It used to be her favourite time of the year, watching Hans at work, trying to look tough and manly with all the elders, while she giggled like the stupid little girl she had sworn she'd never be.

She shook that thought off. Grief was everywhere all the time. It didn't have to be here at the one time she let herself be away from it.

Nearing the forest, she stopped. Somebody was watching her. She turned, arranging her face to give no sign of joy or sadness, no opportunity for anybody to gossip about what her expression might mean.

Somebody was watching her, somebody she saw immediately. From a distance she immediately recognised the tall, thin figure of Samuel. Always strange, always mysterious, barely ever speaking; as children he had been a fascination, as adults he was a curiosity, at all times he was generally avoided. Samuel's quiet intensity and withdrawn nature led to rumours and nobody liked being associated with rumours.

Rebecca refused to look away. She could barely make out his face at this distance, but she prided herself on not being thrown by anyone. And Samuel had always seemed kind to her, even if now she was somewhat unsettled by him. But nonetheless, she held her ground. She would not be the first to scurry away.

Samuel raised a hand and tipped his hat slightly. Then turned on his heel and was gone, almost as suddenly as he had apparently appeared.

It took Rebecca a moment to realise her heart was beating slightly faster. Had the day grown hotter? She shook her head. Strange as Samuel was, she would not let her tiredness exacerbate that. She had no need to be distracted by Samuel of all people when she had promised this time to herself. She turned and kept walking into the trees.

The entire settlement always seemed peaceful, but compared to everything else the forest was the eye of the storm. There was no sign of human interaction, no sign of anything other than serene nature; the gently swaying branches, the scrubby bushes, the tweeting birds and occasional scurrying form of a squirrel.

She glanced behind her. She was deep enough now to see only forest in all directions. She smiled and closed her eyes. Here it was easy to pretend that nothing else existed, that this solitude and sanctuary were everything. If there was no-one else in the world, she couldn't lose anyone ever again.

'Rebecca?'

It was as though somebody had dropped a boulder in calm water. Hearing someone else here was wrong, somehow, as absurd as that thought was. The forest, after all, was free to visit for the entire community. She forced away the anger and turned to face the intruder.

Hands in pockets, Erik stood there, smiling below the wide brim of his hat. Tall, handsome and muscular with the perpetual glint of a joke in his eye, Erik was very well loved in the community. Rebecca quite liked him herself, but at that moment she wasn't predisposed to like anybody, especially not someone who had interrupted her walk.

'Yes?' she said.

'I saw you heading into the forest. I thought I'd see if you were alright.'

'Why wouldn't I be?'

Erik shrugged. 'I don't know. I worry. Everyone worries.'

'There is no need to worry about me,' she said.

'Well it's hardly up to those who need worrying about to decide on the need,' Erik said.

'Maybe it should be,' she replied. 'I don't mean to be rude Erik, but I'm in no mood.'

He nodded. 'That's just it Rebecca. You've been in no mood for a year now. Isn't it time you let somebody talk to you again? You never know; that somebody might be able to make you smile.'

'Would the somebody you refer to be yourself by any chance?'

Erik's smile grew slightly. 'What gave it away?'

'I'm happy not smiling,' Rebecca said. 'If that changes, I'll let you know.'

Erik took a step towards her, his expression growing serious. 'Rebecca, we all miss the frustrating, impetuous girl you used to be.'

'That girl could be frustrating and impetuous,' Rebecca snapped. 'That girl didn't have to care for a sickly mother, didn't have a daughter. That girl hadn't lost...'

Dizziness hit for a moment and was gone. Rebecca took a deep breath. Those moments were fewer and fewer, moments when the weight of Hans' death made her lose balance. A year was a long time in many ways, but in too many others it wasn't nearly long enough.

'How long it takes me to get back to myself is my business and mine alone,' she said. 'I may never be who I was again, and I have come to terms with that. It's time everyone else did too.'

'But we wouldn't be your friends if we accepted that,' Erik said. 'I'm here to help, whether you want me to or not.'

'Ah yes, I do love it when my own desires are not taken into account,' Rebecca said.

'Tomorrow night is the dance,' he said. 'I think you should come.'

Rebecca placed her hands on her hips. 'Is that so?'

Erik nodded. 'Consider it a favour to me.'

'What if I don't want to give you a favour?'

'Then let me offer a favour in return,' he said. 'Come to the dance with me, stay at least an hour, and if you don't like it I will leave you alone. Don't come, and I will take it that you still need help coming back to the world.'

'That's not fair,' she said. 'All I want is to be left alone Erik, is that so great a request? Respecting my wishes should be reason enough.'

'Rebecca.' He paused, watching her. 'Rebecca, what life will you have if you remain alone forever? What life will your daughter have without a father? I know you think you can do it all alone and you probably can, but that does not for a second mean that you *should*. Hans would not want you to spend the rest of your life a lonely widow. You deserve better than that. You deserve happiness and you do not do anyone wrong to allow happiness for yourself. You just have to take the leap.' His smile returned and he tipped his hat. 'I'll be at your house tomorrow evening to see if you want to come to the dance. Please do. Even if there is a very real risk of you enjoying yourself.' With that, he turned and, whistling in a supremely irritating way, headed back out of the forest.

Rebecca watched after him, not moving. Annoying as he was, his words were repeating themselves again and again in his head. *You do not do anyone wrong to allow happiness for yourself.* Was he right? Was she avoiding happiness for fear of dishonouring Hans' memory? The warm day suddenly seemed much colder. It was the kind of thought she preferred to not have to deal with. Perhaps it was true, and perhaps it seemed the right thing to do, but how would she feel looking back in her old age, thinking on all those wasted years? She closed her eyes. Perhaps going to the dance wouldn't be the worst thing. Perhaps.

She took her time heading home. It wasn't a long walk, but she could drag it out if need be, letting herself be distracted by any pretty thing she saw, enjoying the deep breaths of fresh air, staring up into the clear blue sky, wandering along like a daydreaming child. She let any thought enter her mind except those of Erik and the dance. Tomorrow she could think on that. For now, she had gotten away to be thoughtless and she would let herself do exactly that.

Arriving back at her house, she paused on the porch and looked out across the grass, to the distant shapes of the nearest houses, the forest off to the left, the clear blue sky framing it all. She was so very fortunate to live somewhere as beautiful as this, and it would not do to waste that fortune. Life was short and she was surrounded by beauty and good people. Did she have any right not to live when some weren't even given that choice?

It was easier to push that thought away and deal with it later. She opened the door and walked inside. Without Sara here the house seemed still, silent. But her mother should have been up by now. For all her talk of resting, Elsa was rarely tardy. Rebecca frowned.

'Mother?' she called.

No reply. She felt a flicker of concern.

She went straight to the door to her room and pushed it open. Her mother lay on her bed under the blankets, staring up at the roof, blank faced. Something gripped Rebecca's heart and within seconds she was on her knees beside Elsa's bed.

'Mother, wake up,' she said, her heart pounding through the cold vice that had closed around it. 'Mother, please wake up, don't do this, please mother!'

Elsa's chest was rising and falling very slightly. *She was alive.* But why wasn't she replying? Rebecca shook her, gently first then roughly when she didn't rouse or react. Fire and ice were alternating through her veins as images raced through her head, a succession of memories of the moments after Hans' death and flashes of what could be ahead, a life without her mother, another loss to contend with right when she was coming to terms with the first.

Tears in her eyes, breathing ragged, she stumbled back out into the house, bursting through the front door into sunlight that should not still be so warm and pleasant. And she yelled, yelled for someone, anyone, anyone who could come and help. She didn't know how or what they could do and it didn't matter. She just needed somebody.

A shadow fell over her. She looked up. She did not remember falling to her knees. Everything was so blurred and confused.

'What is it?' Samuel asked, no inflection in his voice, no discernible emotion.

'My Mother,' Rebecca managed. Absurdly it occurred to her how much she sounded like a child.

Samuel hurried past her into the house. She forced herself to stand and moments later he had returned, Elsa in his arms as he hurried down the path, past Rebecca. It took her a moment to catch her bearings and hurry after him. She wanted to ask if Elsa would be alright, to ask what he thought, but composure was returning in the face of her need to be calm. Samuel did not know the answers. The doctor would.

They arrived at his small house. Samuel yelled for him and Kai, short, stocky and somewhat round, met them within moments. He directed Samuel to bring Elsa inside and firmly told Rebecca to wait when she tried to follow. Taken aback, she did, only to be joined after a few seconds by Samuel. He met her gaze, they stood like that for a moment, then, without a word, he stepped forward and embraced her.

Was it untoward? Inappropriate? Strange? Yes, but Rebecca did not care. She embraced him back. Comfort was a port in the storm of confusion and fear, and Samuel, at that moment, was the only one offering her comfort. Not the cheap, false comfort of tittered platitudes and whispered enquiries about her wellbeing, but simple, physical presence with no expectation of her saying anything more than she wanted to. He would just be there as long as she needed. Even if she could have spoken, she lacked the words to tell him how grateful she was.

It did not feel like that much time had passed when the door opened and Kai emerged. Rebecca let go of Samuel and turned to face him. He smiled.

'A seizure,' he said. 'Not a serious one. Common, in her condition. I have given her some medication, she will be alright.'

That vice around her heart, familiar from Hans, loosened. She had forgotten it was there. Sometimes you became accustomed to the worst feelings. But that did not matter. Rebecca laughed through renewed tears.

'Thank you doctor,' she said.

'I would like to watch over her a little longer,' Kai said. 'Samuel, take Rebecca home, would you? That was a scare no-one should have.'

Usually Rebecca would have snapped that she could take herself home, but she was too shaken and too grateful to do anything of the sort. So she just nodded, thanked Kai again, and followed Samuel as he began to walk.

In silence they made their way back to her house. The day seemed pleasant again; more than pleasant, beautiful. Relief, Rebecca realised, was the most potent emotion there was, especially when you had been in situations that did not end with it.

'Your mother is a strong woman,' Samuel said finally.

Rebecca nodded. 'Very.'

'It seems that runs in the family.'

She glanced at him, a little confused. 'What do you mean?'

Samuel shrugged. 'You proceed with such dignity, despite losses that would cripple most. But you do not pretend to be happy or ready to move on, despite people's judgements. I think most people going through grief force themselves to smile and move past it so that they can distract themselves, rather than properly dealing with what ails them. You won't distract yourself. You tackle grief head on. I doubt I would have the constitution.'

Rebecca laughed. Relief had the side effect of making you as giddy as a school girl, but she didn't care. 'You? Samuel, you are the toughest person in the community.'

Samuel smiled and Rebecca almost stopped in her tracks. Had she ever seen that before?

'It's funny how fear can be mistaken for many things,' he said. 'No Rebecca, I am not tough at all. Just scared.'

'Scared of what?' she asked, as bemused as she was fascinated.

Samuel paused for a moment. He looked up at the sky, frowning. But if he had wanted to say anything, he gave no sign of it. He kept walking and Rebecca had to hurry to keep up.

They reached the house and came to a halt. Rebecca turned to Samuel, ready to thank him again, but he was already speaking.

'I know Erik wants to convince you to come to the dance,' he said. 'I know he is pressuring you. If you feel you should, then do. But never feel like you must do anything because somebody tells you to. Never.' A ghost of a smile touched his lips, he inclined his head, then with a mumbled good day turned and was on his way again.

Rebecca stared after him. Some strange new feeling had mingled with her relief. Something that was both heavy and light at once, if such a thing were possible. Something that was just making her more confused than ever.

Elsa returned home with Kai later that evening with almost no sign of her ailment. When Sara asked where she had been the old woman made some quip about nosiness being a sin and that she had important business to attend to, which Sara laughed at, leading to a playful argument that had Rebecca smiling as she made dinner.

She had not told her daughter about the day's scare. Rebecca did not want her to fear potentially losing her grandmother as well and besides, Elsa gave no sign of anything being wrong. That old woman would outlive the rest of them.

So the evening progressed normally. The three of them had dinner together and Rebecca said very little, only picking at her food as she looked between her strong, indefatigable mother and her curious, strange daughter. What if today had gone differently? What if only two of them had sat at this dinner table? Rebecca didn't want to think about it, but the image of her mother's blank face staring at the ceiling seemed seared into her memories. That, plus the words of bother Erik and Samuel, meant that she felt well and truly tired and confused by the time she sat down to read Sara's bedtime story.

The tediousness of it seemed more comforting than ever tonight, and by the time the tortoise beat the hare through being slow and steady Rebecca felt more calm than she had all day. She closed the book and looked down at Sara, who was frowning as if deep in thought.

'What is it?' Rebecca asked.

'You didn't sound bored tonight,' Sara said.

Rebecca smiled. Of course she noticed. 'I'm never bored. It's a good story.'

Sara shrugged, but didn't reply.

For a moment, Rebecca considered her child. She felt scared, for some reason. But if anybody knew the right answer, it would be her daughter.

'How would you feel if I married again?' Rebecca asked.

Sara didn't look at her. 'Are you going to marry again?'

Rebecca laughed. 'I would have to have a prospect, which I do not. No, I mean more... if I moved on. Would you feel like I had betrayed your father?'

'Marrying isn't important,' Sara said. 'But moving on is. You'll betray yourself if you don't.' She met her eyes and smiled. 'I miss father every day. You do too. But we are still alive. I don't think there is any point in being alive if all we ever feel is sadness.'

For a moment neither of them spoke as Rebecca considered her words.

'You're clever, Sara,' she said, after a few moments.

'I know, Sara said.

Rebecca kissed her daughter on the head, then bid her goodnight. She put out the candles and walked out through the still kitchen and into her bedroom. She dressed for bed and then lay down, in her bed which had felt far too big for her for so long. It was always as though she was enveloped in more space than she needed here, and perhaps that was why she barely slept anymore.

But tonight, as she lay down and closed her eyes, she drifted off within moments.

She dreamed of Hans, as handsome and happy and full of life as he had been on their wedding day. She dreamed of dancing together with him below a starry sky. There was no-one else in the world, just the two of them, just that feeling of safety, of home and love and joy. But the music slowed and the dance stopped and Hans, with one last smile, kissed her on the cheek then turned and walked away into the night and Rebecca watched him go but did not call after him, just let him keep walking until the dark swallowed him up and she was alone with the stars.

For the first time in a long time she paid close attention to getting dressed, to ensuring that she looked meticulous. Elsa helped her with her hair and when she looked in the mirror she felt like she was that beautiful young woman again whom everyone had despaired of and loved in equal measure. For a moment, it took her breath away. She turned to her mother. Elsa smiled and kissed her on the head without a word and Rebecca *felt* like that little girl again. But she was no little girl. She was a grown woman.

She met Erik at the front door, meeting his smile with her own. He offered his arm and she took it. Together they walked into the evening.

Was she scared? Perhaps. Excited? It was hard to tell. But whatever strange mix of emotions she felt, it was more than the emptiness that had been her lot for too long now, and that was enough. Erik was talking about something and she smiled and nodded and laughed when he made what sounded like jokes, but she wasn't listening. Her mind was on the terrifying yet exhilarating idea that maybe this could be the beginning of something, the beginning of a real return to herself.

It took seeing the church hall for fear to outweigh everything else. The very image of people milling around out the front reminded her starkly of Hans' funeral and involuntarily her hand tightened around Erik's arm.

'It's alright,' he said. 'I'm here.'

Was that comforting? She didn't know. But she didn't relinquish her grip. Together they approached the doors.

The moment she walked through she could feel eyes on her, from all directions. Were they muttering? Was she hearing her name echoed back at her as people tittered and gossiped? She tried to tell herself she didn't care but this spacious hall felt so much more claustrophobic than the safety of her home had in the last year.

She glanced at Erik, but he wasn't paying attention to her. He was smiling around at everyone and she felt a twinge of discomfort. There was precious little excitement left in how she felt about tonight.

'Excuse me,' she muttered, letting go or Erik and heading straight for a table off to the side. She needed a glass of water and jugs had been left out, surrounded by platters of food. She felt hot, like all the eyes on her were burning. Was it in her head, or was everyone staring at her?

With a trembling hand she poured a glass and gulped it back, then another.

'What are you doing?'

She turned. Erik was standing behind her, looking concerned.

'I need a drink.' She tried to keep calm.

'You look upset.'

'I'm not upset.'

'Rebecca, everyone is here. Everyone is looking. You're flustered.'

'Well you're not helping,' she snapped, and pushed past him to be met with a flock of faces that she knew were familiar but none of whom she could name. Women she had grown up with, had been friends with, the very women she dreaded seeing in the months since she lost Hans.

'Rebecca, are you–'

'You seem–'

'It's so good to see you tonight–'

'Are you here with Erik?'

'Has he asked–'

'When he said you were coming I didn't–'

Rebecca closed her eyes and tried to steady her breathing. 'Please, just let me be.'

'Rebecca is alright,' Erik announced, taking her arm again. 'Go and enjoy the dance.'

She felt herself being guided away, then Erik took her arm and she looked up into his eyes.

'Get yourself together,' he hissed.

'I want to go home.'

'You are embarrassing me,' Erik said. 'Really Rebecca, enough is enough. You can't keep acting in this way, demanding everyone's attention, humiliating the people who try–'

'That is enough.'

The voice came from behind them. Rebecca and Erik turned at the same time to see Samuel standing there, face impassive, hands by his sides. But his eyes...

'What do you want?' Erik asked. 'We are talking.'

'She does not seem to be enjoying the conversation,' Samuel replied.

Erik let go of her and took a step towards Samuel. A hush had fallen over the hall. Now Rebecca *knew* everyone was looking. But she only had eyes for Samuel, standing alone and calm.

'Her happiness is none of your business,' Erik said.

'And it is yours?'

Erik looked Samuel up and down with a sneer. 'Go home Samuel. Nobody wants you here.'

'I do,' Rebecca said.

Erik did not even look at her. 'Be quiet Rebecca,' he said. 'This is between–'

It seemed to happen so slowly, and yet it was over in seconds. Samuel stepped forward and at the same moment his fist sent Erik flying.

'I said that's enough.' Samuel said, as Erik hit the floor with a yelp and several cries went up around the hall. Samuel did not seem to care though. He looked at Rebecca.

She smiled.

Together they walked for the door. People parted as if they were dangerous or contagious, their mouths gaping and their eyes wide, but for the first time she didn't care at all.

They emerged into the cool night air. Rebecca started walking back towards her house, and part of her expected Samuel to stop, but he didn't. Together they walked in silence under the starry sky and Rebecca did not stop smiling until they arrived at her front door.

She turned to face Samuel. For a moment they just stood there in the cool night air looking at each other.

'Nobody has any right to tell you who you should be or how you should feel,' he said.

'I know,' she replied.

For a few seconds all that could be heard was the wind in the trees of the distant forest.

'Thank you,' she said.

He nodded.

'Would you like to come in for a cup of tea?' she said.

Samuel didn't speak. He just smiled. Her own smile grew.

The night had gotten warmer.

The End

THE AMISH BAKER

GABRIELA BELL

I

Hildegard missed her grandfather. Had it really been two years since his passing? she wondered. It seemed hardly a week ago she had knelt by his bed sobbing as he drew his final breaths. On the other hand, so much had happened since that it felt like a lifetime ago. He had been her only refuge since she could remember, and now she felt knocked about by the world with nothing to hold onto.

Hildegard had never known her parents, who had died before her third birthday. Her long-widowed grandfather was living with them when it happened and only reluctantly found himself saddled with the child. Though he was prone to complaints and a cloudy disposition, he grew to love his granddaughter as his own, and of all his various relatives he looked upon her most favorably as a kindred spirit. Even in her infancy everyone had noted the resemblance in their respective characters. She was solemn child, seldom excited, never rowdy or rambunctious, with an air of the tragic as if she had inherited the deep, weary sadness which seemed to haunt her grandfather.

It had been many years when his daughter and son-in-law died since the old man had raised a child, but the memories quickly came flooding back to him like a second nature. Hildegard was six when he taught her how to bake bread. She had enjoyed it so much that the old man made sure she kept at it and refined her skill. Most of her best memories of her grandfather involved explosions of flour, glowing hot ovens, and long hours of kneading dough. He was stern, and occasionally lost his patience with her, but he loved the craft and his granddaughter dearly and endured her childish mistakes for their sakes.

By the time Hildegard came of age she was the best baker in the village, second only to her grandfather, who had given up the trade in order to make room for Hildegard. He had taught her well everything she needed to know to become one of the feminine pillars of the community. She was fluent in both English and their dialect of German (though the former she had learned with some difficulty since her grandfather barely spoke it).

He had instructed her in the Law and the Prophets: how Eve had enticed Adam with the forbidden fruit after being deceived by the serpent, how Adam had consigned his descendants to everlasting death through his sin, how Hildegard, her grandfather, and every other human being to have ever lived was laid under this curse. And he had instructed her in the call of the Gospel: how God had sent his son Jesus Christ to atone for the sins of the world, trampling under foot death and the devil, and how it was her duty to believe on the Lord Jesus for her salvation and to love him above all things and love her neighbor as herself.

He had taught her the duties of a good wife, her place in the community, and the dignity of motherhood. In all things both spiritual and temporal his education was impeccable, so that in her blossoming womanhood she looked forward equally to her wedding day and that dread day when the heavens would open up and the Lord Jesus would usher the righteous into the life of the world to come. She saw history condensed into one timeless moment, and it was her highest aspiration to be a part of that mystery of love.

She was also well aware of the dangers of the world, of the masses who lived in sin with no knowledge of the Savior, who were beguiled by the arrogant devices of men, who preferred lavish comfort to the simple, quiet life. There was no hatred of the "English", as those in her village called them, only a deep pity for their poor souls, and a vague suspicion of their intentions whenever her people encountered them. She knew they did not understand her way of life, and that it was useless to try and prove her election to them.

With her grandfather to support her, Hildegard felt safe and content in her tiny world. It was a good life – simple, slow, peaceful, and contemplative. She was fifteen when the old man's age started to catch up with him. He had kept active in the twilight of his life, and was for the most part was no worse for ware. But eventually he began to slow down. His joints began to ache and ossify, especially his knees, which made it hard for him to get up and down. A cough settled in his lungs and lingered. For three years he deteriorated, first incrementally, and then all at once.

One morning he was too weak to get out of bed. Hildegard sent for Dr. Morgenstern who said there was nothing left to be done, that he would probably be dead before the week was out. And on the eve of her eighteenth birthday, she knelt by his side and waited for that dreadful silence to fall upon him.

"Do stop whimpering," the old man said to her at length. "One would think you a pagan, mourning for my death because you have no hope. Be joyful, and do not wail with grief like the English. Now leave me in peace."

That was the last thing he said to her. He died in the early hours of the morning. Not having a husband, Hildegard went to live with her next of kin: an uncle on the other side of the county. Now she had lived there for two years, and on the eve of her twentieth birthday she bustled about the kitchen, trying to distract herself from her thoughts with the production of a birthday cake. Her friends had family had long conceded that the only baker whose skill could possible satisfy Hildegard was Hildegard herself, and so they allowed her to bake her own cakes even on her own birthdays.

Hildegard missed her grandfather something awful. And her present company did not help to alleviate her nostalgia. Her uncle Wilhelm had, like her, inherited his father's gloomy and sour attitude, but unfortunately none of his compassion or enduring love. He was just a grump, and was apt to fall into fits of evil temper. Hildegard was suspicious, too, of his piety. She had heard stories that in his youth he had been less than dedicated to the demands of their religion, and had very nearly been shunned.

Apparently his *rumspringa* had stretched the limits of acceptable adolescent misbehavior, and it was only after his father had consented to give his blessing to the marriage of Wilhelm to the young maiden of his choice that he had been baptized in the church. Since these unhappy days, Wilhelm had lived a quiet life and kept out of trouble, but there were nasty rumors that he still occasionally fraternized with less than wholesome characters among the English. Hildegard felt guilty that she did not entirely disbelieve them.

Wilhelm had accepted Hildegard into his home because he knew it was his duty, but he was not happy about it.

"We must see to it that you are married soon," he said upon her arrival. She had smiled, but he did not return it. There was a haughtiness in his eyes, and a bitterness that his life had not gone all as he had wanted it. To him she was just another burden, another girl to wash his hands of as quickly as possible.

Her aunt Marta was pleasant enough, but she was passive and turned a blind eye to her husband's cruelty. Whatever love had once existed between Marta and Wilhelm seemed to have evanesced long ago. Now he ignored her and she feared him. Once Marta had been helping Hildegard in the kitchen and had accidentally broken an egg on the floor. Wilhelm, returning from a hard day's work in the fields, had entered the house, taken one look at the mess and smacked his wife across the face. It was a shock to Hildegard, who all her life had understood and upheld the Lord's call to non-violence, but Marta shrugged and said, "Men . . ." They never spoke of this incident again.

Hildegard knew that her uncle was busy about finding her a husband, but after nearly two years the lucky gentleman had not materialized. It seemed Hildegard was too cold, too austere, even for the devout Mennonite men in her village. Wilhelm grew more and more sour towards her as he realized she was a problem he was not going to be able to shake easily.

Once, in a moment of relative candor, Wilhelm had sat down across the dinner table from her and squinted meanly.

"I would have better luck getting you wed if you were English," he grunted, and then he lumbered off to bed.

But on the morning of her twentieth birthday, everything changed.

Wilhelm had delayed going to the fields. Normally, he was out of the house by five o'clock, but when Hildegard went to the kitchen to make breakfast at seven, he was sitting at the table smirking.

"Happy birthday," he said.

Hildegard was surprised. It was not like Wilhelm to even remember birthdays other than his own, let alone mention them out loud.

"Thank you." She curtsied and went about her work.

"Leave that!" he ordered. "Have a seat."

She did as she was told.

"I have good news for you for your birthday," Wilhelm said.

Hildegard was silent. She had a feeling she knew what was coming.

"I believe I have found a suitable husband for you."

She clenched her jaw, but said nothing.

"He is a friend of mine. He wants to meet you. I thought it would be a good idea to invite him to dinner tonight."

Hildegard knew she ought to be happy, but the persistent smirk on her uncle's face made her cautious.

"You will meet with him?" he said.

Hildegard pursed her lips and thought. "Very well," she said. "Only, what is his name?"

"Jakob Lippmann," said her uncle.

She nodded. She recognized the name, but could not recall his face nor any other detail about him. He must be older, she thought. Her mind went over what sort of man this might be whom her uncle had chosen for her. Perhaps he was a good, pious, hard-working man. But her uncle had tried to betroth her to several good, pious, hard-working men, and they had all recoiled at her harsh demeanor. Wilhelm was desperate to have her off his hands, she knew, which meant he was likely to offer her to anyone who would take her. Perhaps this Jacob Lippmann was also undesirable. That her uncle said he was a friend of his concerned her, considering the kind of company he used to keep. But she knew it was a sin to pre-judge her fellow men, so she resolved not to think poorly of this apparently ready and willing suitor until she knew more about him.

From time to time, Hildegard still encountered some of her childhood friends. She saw Mrs. Strusse, Abigail, a woman one year her junior, at the market. They had been neighbors when Hildegard had lived with her grandfather. Now Abigail was very happily married to a tailor.

"Happy birthday, Hilde," Abigail said in greeting.

"Thank you," said Hildegard.

She told Abigail the news.

"That is splendid, Hilde. You should give thanks to God."

True enough, Hildegard thought, but she said, "I know the name, Jakob Lippmann, but I do not know anything about the man."

"You are to be married to Jakob Lippmann?" said Mrs. Strusse.

"If my uncle has his way."

Abigail frowned.

"What is it?" asked Hildegard.

"It seems a curious choice. He must be nearly twice your age."

Hildegard had assumed he must be older since her uncle claimed the man as a friend.

"What else do you know about him?"

Abigail shrugged and cast her eyes to the floor. "It is not good to discuss the affairs of others when not in their presence."

Hildegard raised her eyebrows. "He is my affair now!" she said. "If you have some knowledge to impart, please do not hesitate."

Abigail sighed. "You may find out from him yourself in time."

"Abigail!" said Hildegard. "Abigail, my old friend. I must know what sort of man this is I am to marry, since it seems I will have little say in the matter. I am a burden to my uncle, and I dare not refuse whatever arrangements he will make. Do you not see my need?"

Abigail frowned and thought. Finally, reluctantly, she said, "All right. I don't want you to think ill of him because of what I have said, but his name is mildly infamous I'm afraid."

"Go on."

"I cannot say too much, for it was many years ago, but it is said that the elders look for any excuse to shun him. There are rumors that he brews liquor in his barn and sells it to the English. I know for a fact that during his *rumspringa* he spent a night in an English jail cell."

"Why?" Hildegard was amazed.

Abigail lowered her voice and whispered. "*Fighting!*"

"And he has not been excommunicated?" Hildegard was incredulous.

"They have never caught him," said Abigail. "Maybe none of the rumors are true, but I say it makes you wonder."

"Fascinating."

Abigail was not happy with her friend. "We have sinned, Hildegard. It is wicked to besmirch a man's reputation thus."

"But I thank you all the same," said Hildegard. "I must know what kind of man my husband is to be."

"Are we his judges?" said Abigail. "We presume to know his heart? This is not good, Hildegard. This is *hochmut*."

"I do not desire to know his heart. Only the worth of his actions."

"May God have mercy on us. Good day, Hildegard." Abigail hustled out of the store as if pursued by the devil. Hildegard was not proud of herself, but she did not feel guilty either. I had to know, she thought.

So this is what her uncle had devised for her – a marriage of convenience to one of his old cohorts, a ruffian, prone to violence. It made her sick. Yet still she was not entirely surprised. Despite all of this, she knew better than to rush to any absolute judgments about the man. She would give him a chance at dinner and see if he really was what he appeared to be.

I suppose I really have no right to complain, she thought. If I had been a little kinder, smiled more, not been so severe, maybe young men my age would have taken interest in me. It was an uncomfortable thought, but Hildegard had to admit the truth of it. This whole situation was her fault. She had put herself in this situation, and now she had to reap what she sowed.

Mr. Jakob Lippmann arrived for dinner at six o'clock. Wilhelm greeted him at the door while Marta and Hildegard watched from the kitchen. From the look of it, Mr. Lippmann was a year or two younger than Wilhelm. He had a long brown beard, and bits of grey were already starting to show.

"I'm so sorry dear," whispered Marta. Hildegard felt a dull ache begin to form in her stomach.

Marta had fixed a pork tenderloin for dinner, and Hildegard had made some biscuits. At dinner, Wilhelm led the prayer.

"We thanks thee for thy bounty O Jesus Christ. May it strengthen us to do thy will in all things. Amen."

"Wilhelm tells me this is your twentieth birthday," said Mr. Lippmann.

Hildegard nodded. "Indeed it is, sir."

Mr. Lippmann laughed. "I see why it has taken her so many years to find a husband."

Hildegard blushed. The impertinence of the man. Her grandfather would have defended her honor. Once again she missed him fiercely.

Mr. Lippmann ate voraciously and chewed with his mouth open. He spoke to Hildegard through a piece of pig meat.

"We are both very lucky to have your uncle. I am afraid neither one of us has many prospects."

Hildegard kept her peace. She did not bite back. She did not glare at him. But in her heart she begrudged him the comment.

Marta spoke up. "Hildegard made the biscuits."

Mr. Lippmann tasted one. "Well," he shrugged, "I suppose there's room for improvement on both sides."

Hildegard was not proud of her skill in baking. She gave thanks to God for the gift, but there was no need for the insult. She felt justified now in her indignation. She wished her grandfather had arranged for her wedding before he had passed. She simply could not marry this buffoon.

"I shan't do it!" she told her uncle the next morning.

"You shall. What choice do you have?"

"I cannot. He is a beast of a man. He is more disagreeable than you, dear uncle."

"I will not have you before me in that manner."

"I have tried to be as respectful as I can, uncle, considering my lowly state, but this marriage I cannot and will not abide. It would be a sin."

"It would be sin to refuse. I'll not continue to shelter you indefinitely. I had my own children. You are a dependent. You will marry Jakob, or I shall turn you out, regardless of what the elders say. You cannot live alone without a husband."

Marta observed and said nothing.

And so Hildegard was faced with a decision. To marry Mr. Lippmann and stay with her people, whom she loved, whose religion she shared, whose way of life was all she had ever known, or to leave it all behind and risk a chance at happiness. It was a week after her birthday that she packed up her belongings and left in the middle of the night. The tears flowing down her cheeks stung her skin as they froze in the cold air of winter...

II

At five thirty on a Thursday morning, Hildegard rose from her bed. She switched on the light in the bathroom and set about readying herself for a good day's work. She washed her face and took a hot shower. Though every fiber of her being rejected it, she touched up her cheeks with a little rouge and made sure her lips did not appear too dry or bland.

Dressed for work in a pink t-shirt and blue jeans, her hair up in a pony-tail, Hildegard stood over the kitchen sink and munched on a slice of toast which she had heated in an electric toaster. Three months before, she had used an electric toaster for the first time. She half-expected the earth to split open beneath her and swallow her into the everlasting lake of fire – and she would have deserved it, she thought.

In the early morning twilight, satisfying her hunger, Hildegard watched the lightening of the earth through a window. She thought of the Lord Jesus, who set the earth on its foundation, put the stars in motion, and made the sun to know the time of its setting. Did he know her pain, her loss, her sense of abandon? Yes. He knew. And she prayed he would not reprobate her forever.

At seven she arrived at the bakery and unlocked the doors. She waited for Bohdan to arrive and fire up the ovens. Bohdan was the son of the owner, an English baker named Jaroslav Danilo. Only he was not actually English, she remembered. He was an immigrant from Trans-Carpathia, an outsider like herself. He attended one of those onion-domed churches across the State line. Everything around her reminded her she was a stranger in a strange land.

I will live as the English live, she told herself, but I will not adopt their ways into my heart.

When she had to use electricity she gritted her teeth and bore the indignity. She wore contemporary clothing begrudgingly, but satisfied herself that she made sure the colors were not too bright and the cuts not too ostentatious. Every day was a challenge to endure. What she could not get used to, what she could not abide, was the noise. The English world was so noisy. The bakery played songs from the radio from opening at eight 'til closing at six. Alone in her house, Hildegard was ever aware of the sounds of traffic racing by outside and the television in her neighbor's house blaring. Now she knew what it felt like to hallucinate, to be constantly bombarded with empty sensory stimulation. How did they live like this?

Occasionally she saw her people about in the town, riding their horse-drawn buggies to the general store or to sell eggs and jams in the markets. Once or twice they came into the bakery, and Hildegard found an excuse to retreat into the pantry or the loading dock. It was prideful, she knew, to be so ashamed, but she simply could not face them.

She started working at the bakery a week into her new English life.

"I have no need for Amish baker girl!" Jaroslav said when she asked for the job.

She had brought a loaf of sourdough with her to the bakery which she had baked at home.

"Very well," she said. "Thank you for your time. Please take this gift of my appreciation." She left the sourdough with him.

The next day Jaroslav met her on the street and begged her to come work for him. Of course she agreed. Bohdan resented her. Compared to Hildegard he was a novice at baking. But Jaroslav had set him straight and commanded him to be gracious to her. So now the young man tried his best not to have to speak to her, but the threat of his father's wrath kept him from being too terribly harsh.

It was a good way to make a living, she thought. But what good is it for a man to gain the whole world and lose his soul?

On this particular day, business was relatively slow. The bakery was empty, save for Bohdan and Hildegard, until nine thirty. Hildegard was tending to a batch of blueberry muffins when she heard the little bell ring which signals that someone had entered the bakery.

Hildegard went out into the store and stood behind the counter, ready to wait on the customer. She stopped short when she saw Mr.

Jakob Lippmann standing there examining the scones. When he looked up and saw her he shook his head, as if unsure that he actually recognized her. They stared at each other for a pregnant moment, until Hildegard finally said, "How can I help you, sir?"

Mr. Lippmann said, "Wilhelm's niece, correct?"

Hildegard sighed. She had hoped he would whistle past the graveyard as she had.

"Yes, Mr. Lippmann. That is right," she said.

"Everyone is very worried about you," he said.

"I find that hard to believe. What do you need?"

Mr. Lippmann sighed. "I need a loaf of sourdough and a blueberry muffin, if you please."

Hildegard reached for a bag and grabbed the tongs from the counter. She set the loaf of sourdough inside and was about to do the same when Mr. Lippmann stopped her.

"No need to bag the muffin, miss," he said. "It is only for me."

She narrowed her eyes at him. "As you wish, sir."

"I assume you made them."

"Yes, sir." Would he insult her baking again? What was he up to?

"The village has been sorely wanted for good baking since you left. Mrs. Strusse has had to accommodate them."

She gave him the muffin.

"Thank you," he said. He took a bight and smiled. "Heavenly as always."

Hildegard took a breath. He was so polite. What kind of deception was he about? she wondered.

"Thank you, sir," she said.

He paid her and took his bread. When he got to the door she called after him.

"Mr. Lippman!" she yelled. He turned around and looked at her, saying nothing. "I would appreciate it if you do not tell them where I am or what I am doing."

He thought a moment, then bowed. "If you wish it, so shall it be." Then he left. The little bell rang again. Hildegard heard the clop clopping of horse's hooves outside. Then she went back to her batch of muffins.

III

Jakob Lippmann was sixteen-years-old when he was arrested by the highway patrol for fighting with an English farmer over a girl. He spent two nights in jail before his parents were able to bail him out. Fortunately, his friend Wilhelm was present when the arrest took place, otherwise his family might not have known what happened to him for days.

He was let go on probation. The elders of the church were less understanding, however, than the State of Pennsylvania. Though they did not excommunicate him, the community looked upon him as a trouble maker, as one who had disregarded the call of the Gospel and publically scandalized the church. No fathers would allow him to court their daughters, even after he was finally baptized at eighteen.

His crimes were far less severe than those of his friend Wilhelm, but Wilhelm had been clever enough not to get caught, and he had been able to leverage his father's desire for Wilhelm to remain in the church in his favor. Jakob was not so lucky. Where Wilhelm was able to rehabilitate his reputation, Jakob was remembered as a rapscallion, though at heart he was more faithful than Wilhelm.

Few in the village patronized his shop, so he took to brewing moonshine secretly and selling it to the English, though he himself never took a sip. Only Wilhelm remained on good terms with him, and even this relationship was strained, for though Jakob would never vocalize such judgment, he blamed his choice of bad company with Wilhelm for the tarnishing of his good name. Over the years he began to lose hope. He grew sad and bitter. He knew what his church and his God commanded, but they did not make it easy to obey.

Then one day Wilhelm came to him with an idea.

"As you know," said Wilhelm, "I take care of my niece Hildegard. She is very pious, very plain, but as strong-willed as any English woman. I am afraid no young men have taken an interest in her. I cannot say I blame them."

Here Wilhelm chuckled. Jakob did not even smile.

"Since you are getting along in years, Jakob, I thought I might do my old friend a favor. She must be married soon or she will use up all my livelihood."

Oh you foolish, foolish man, thought Jakob. What kind of man would treat his own flesh and blood so scornfully? What kind of man would dare to disrespect a woman in this fashion?

But to Wilhelm he said only, "I should very much like to meet her."

IV

Needless to say, Hildegard was confused. She thought she knew what sort of life she was running away from. She thought she knew the kind of man her husband was to be. But her encounter with Mr. Lippmann on Thursday had her still pondering it on Friday night after work. Hildegard munched on a biscuit and arranged her thoughts.

Several questions presented themselves to her without answers. Why had he been so polite, meek, and complimentary on Thursday? If his nature was to be mean, rude, and impious like her uncle, why would he act differently among the English? And if his nature really was to be meek and gentle, why had he been so rude and uncharitable when they had first met? What exactly was his relationship with her uncle?

Hildegard mulled it over, but no solution materialized.

Within the week she saw him again. And again the week after that. Was he making an effort to see her? she wondered. They made small talk, but Hildegard made very sure not to let her guard down, not to let any sign of weakness cross her bony, stone cold face. She wanted to ask him what the meaning of his behavior was, why he had changed his behavior so drastically. She also wanted to know if the rumors about his *rumspringa* and about his alleged business selling alcohol to the English were true, but she knew that would be highly impertinent.

She found herself anticipating his weekly visits to the bakery. On the few occasions he did not come, she was surprised to find herself disappointed. They continued thusly for maybe two months. One Thursday, Mr. Lippmann entered the shop.

"How can I help you today, Mr. Lippmann?" she asked.

His face was long and grave.

"I do not need to buy anything, Hildegard," he said.

She studied his physiognomy, looking for some sign which would betray his purpose. She found none, so she broke down and asked.

"What is the matter, Mr. Lippmann? Why have you come?"

"It is your uncle. Wilhelm. He is dead."

"What?" said Hildegard. "When? How?"

Mr. Lippmann sighed and hesitated.

"Mr. Lippmann?"

Finally, he spoke. "It was an English farmer. It seems he came home and found your uncle..." he trailed off.

"Yes?" goaded Hildegard.

"He found your uncle with his wife. Do you understand me, Hildegard?"

Hildegard thought. She did understand. And she was not surprised.

"Yes. I think I do."

"The English farmer shot him." Mr. Lippmann cast his eyes to the floor and shook his head. "God have mercy on him."

Hildegard was shocked, but she kept her composure.

"I thought," said Mr. Lippmann, "I thought that you ought to know."

"Thank you," said Hildegard quietly. "Poor Aunt Marta!"

"She is inconsolable."

A silence descended between them. The radio hummed quietly.

At length, Hildegard said, "Well, I thank you again for telling me. Goodbye, Mr. Lippmann."

Mr. Lippmann bowed and headed for the door. The little bell chimed as he stepped outside. Hildegard watched him go anxiously. But she could no longer live in the dark. She had to know. She ran outside after him calling, "Wait! Jakob! Wait!"

He stood by his buggy and turned to see her approaching.

"Hildegard?" he said.

"God forgive me! I have sinned against you!" she exclaimed.

"What is the matter, Hildegard?"

"I left because of you! I thought you were rude and impious like my uncle. I would not be married to a man like him. I am sorry I judged you so harshly!" Hildegard was on the verge of tears.

Mr. Lippmann responded in a soft, gentle voice. "There is no need to apologize. You judged me exactly as I hoped you would. And at one time in my life you would have judged correctly."

Hildegard did not understand him at all.

"What do you mean? Exactly as you hoped I would?"

Mr. Lippmann sighed. "Understand me. I am grateful for your uncle's friendship all these years, but I know as well as anyone that he was not a good man, neither in action nor in his heart of hearts. I am getting older, Hildegard, and I would delight in a wife and the prospect of children, but I knew that your uncle must have had some ulterior motive. He never did anything out of goodness alone."

"I don't follow, Jakob," said Hildegard.

"I did not want it on my conscience that I took advantage of the plight of a young woman. So I made a fool of myself. I knew a woman of your upbringing would refuse the marriage. I did not know that Wilhelm would be so insistent. It is my fault you were forced to flee."

Hildegard was silent. She searched in vain for the proper way to react to such an amazing statement.

"Do not lower your gaze," said Mr. Lippmann. Hildegard looked up at him. "You are very strong, Hildegard. You have the resolve of the matriarch Rachel, and the discretion of Deborah the judge about you."

He mounted the buggy and rode away. Hildegard stood on the busy English sidewalk and watched him go. What have I done? she thought...

It was clear to Hildegard that she may very well have made a mistake when she ran away. Mr. Lippmann did not come the next week, nor the week after that. Now that she knew him better, perhaps he would make a good match for her. In all his dealings with her, limited though they were, he had selflessly put her wellbeing ahead of his, even denied himself the happiness of a wife for her sake. But now she was uncertain of what to do. Could she ever show her face in the village again? If she begged, would the elders accept her back into the church. She could not live there without a husband, and Mr. Lippmann was the only man who had ever humored the slightest suggestion of marrying her. She wanted to despair.

She knelt by her bed and beseeched the Lord her God, asking him for guidance, for she could not discern his will in her life. It was late, past midnight. The house was quiet, as quiet as it ever got among the English. She lay her head on the mattress and wept.

"Oh Lord Jesus," she whispered. "I do not know what to do. I have no one, and nowhere to call home."

Words failed her, and she lay motionless, wishing the night would envelop her and bring her to oblivion.

It was hours of darkness that she sat there on her knees, drifting to and fro on the plane between sleep and wakefulness. And then she heard it: a tiny, tiny whisper, soft and soothing, yet somehow louder and clearer than any voice she had ever heard.

"Why are you crying, Hilde?"

Hildegard did not budge, but answered in her mind: Because I am lost, and I do not know how to return.

"What is it you fear?" asked the voice.

That they will reject me as I rejected them.

"Have you no faith? Do you not trust that I will work the good for those who love me?"

Hildegard did not respond.

The voice continued, "You are powerless, but I am mighty, enthroned above the ages. I have made my enemies my footstool, and yet you still doubt me. My grace is sufficient for you, for my power is perfected in weakness."

Then she slept.

V

In the morning, Hildegard packed her belongings. She left her English clothes behind and proudly wore her frock and bonnet. Then, suitcase in hand, she walked the miles back to the village. It took all day.

As the sun set over the green Pennsylvania field, Hildegard marveled at the beauty of her savior's world. The sky changed from blue to yellow, to bright pink and red, then faded to indigo and violet. Soon the world around her was shadows. The moon was bright white, stars began to show themselves, and the light in the west grew dimmer and dimmer. Hildegard wanted to weep for her pride, her presumption in judging such a good and decent man. But instead she smiled with the joy of her forgiveness.

The air grew cold, and she shivered.

It was eight o'clock when she reached the porch of the house which was her destination. She knocked on the door. When it opened, Mr. Jakob Lippmann stood at the threshold.

"Hildegard?" he said incredulously.

"Yes," she gritted her teeth and tried not to cry. "I have come back Jakob."

After a pause, he said, "Why?"

"Because of you."

"Excuse me?"

"You have been good to me. And if you are still willing to have children, then I am willing to be your bride."

Jakob stared at her, his brows furled.

"You have proven yourself to be a selfless and pious man. Then under God I pray enough of love will follow to make us one flesh."

Jakob was quiet for a long time. Crickets chirped in the fields. A gentle breeze blew the tall grass.

"Hildegard," Jakob started.

"What?" she was too anxious to let him finish.

"Hildegard, the elders will never accept this. You are an apostate."

"Then I shall beg," she announced with fortitude. "The Lord has assured me of the outcome. This is his divine and sovereign will."

Another long silence from Jakob.

He took a deep breath and sighed. "Very well," he said. "So shall it be." He smiled, then gently he kissed her on the cheek. "But you cannot stay here tonight. I must take you to your aunt's."

"Of course."

And he did just that. They were married before the end of the month and had six children. Jakob died at the age of eighty-five, many years later, his wife by his bedside. But for her husband Hildegard did not weep as the pagans do, who have no hope. She was joyful. And her husband left her in peace.

AMISH GIRL IN THE BIG APPLE

ABBY BARKER

It had taken months of begging and pleading to Mama and Papa, but they finally gave in. Ever since she was a little girl, Abby had an obsession with New York City. There was something about its bustling streets, towering buildings, and even its grit and grime that was so opposite to her small Amish community out in the countryside that unrelentingly called out to her. Each time her family passed through neighboring towns on their way to some market or trade show, she'd soak up every billboard and image depicting the towering skyline of the city that never sleeps.

Abby's parents always thought of her fascination with the city as a passing phase, something all young girls go through in some form or another, but once she turned sixteen she began talking more seriously about leaving home. Mama and Papa went away on rumspringa themselves when they were around her age, but they were still nervous thinking about their only daughter running off to the big city. At first, they insisted she pick a smaller, less intimidating city to visit, like Philadelphia or even Chicago where they had family that could keep on eye on her, but Abby was relentless. They tried to convince her to wait until her younger cousin was old enough to go with her to no avail. Abby had been waiting to go to New York City for as long as she could remember and once she turned eighteen she decided she couldn't wait a single second longer.

That morning, bags packed and dressed for travel, Abby sat down at the breakfast table and told her parents that she was leaving that day, with or without their permission. Not wanting to harbor any ill feelings toward their daughter or to explain to their neighbors that she ran off against their wishes, Mama and Papa gave in with a collective defeated sigh. Abby jumped up like a shot and hugged both her parents at once, almost knocking them to the floor.

"Thank you, thank you, thank you! I promise I'll be okay. Sarah's cousin has an apartment in Manhattan and she said I could stay with her for as long as I want and you don't even have to worry about money because Sarah says everyone in New York serving food at restaurants and it would be super easy for me to get a job, even without any experience or anything. I'll write to you every day, or every other day, or when I have time. It's New York, after all. I'm going to have so much to do! It's all so exciting!"

Abby flashed her parents a bright, enthusiastic smile that they tried to replicate, but their nerves stood in the way. Sarah was Abby's best friend from school. Her parents never let her go on rumspringa because of her cousin, Grace. Grace left home to visit the city when she was eighteen and never came back. Sarah's family was devastated, but Sarah kept in touch with Grace and was assured that she was happy and had made the right choice. Sarah's parents didn't want to take the risk that she might do the same.

"Just...be careful. Remember what you have waiting for you back at home."

"Listen to your Mama. This will always be your home. God has a path set for you here."

Abby brushed off her parents' words of caution with a closed-lipped smile and a small shrug. She understood their concern, but a week, or month, or year in New York wouldn't change her fundamental beliefs, and if it did would that automatically be a bad thing? Grace has lived in New York and away from the church for five years now and she was still a good person. Why did being Amish mean she had to hide herself away from the rest of the world her whole life? If she didn't go see the city she's dreamed of her entire life now then she never would. Besides, she was pretty sure she'd come back home. Her parents shouldn't worry so much.

Mama and Papa insisted she stay for one last meal before she caught the bus one town over that said "New York City" on the front. Abby could barely sit still long enough to bring bites of food to her mouth without shaking them off her fork. She'd seen that bus come and go hundreds of times, but that was the day she'd be going with it. Her mother tried to keep up a normal conversation, but Abby could only respond with "yes" or "no." Her mind was officially elsewhere. Eventually her father excused her from the table and she almost ran right out the door, but a small pang in her stomach stopped her at the threshold. Abby was unquestionably excited to start her journey, but she realized that she would miss her parents along the way. She slowed down for a moment to hug them both goodbye.

"Mama, Papa, I love you both very much. I'll see you when I get back."

She added that last part mostly to reassure her parents, but also a little bit for herself. She'd always imagines what might happen if she decided to stay in New York. She'd work hard to become an actress on Broadway, and one night a handsome fan would come to her dressing room after a particularly stirring performance and confess his love for her. It would turn out that he came from a rich family, of course, and even though she could absolutely support herself being a successful actress and all, she'd be in love and carefree for the rest of her life in a Manhattan penthouse. That was all a harmless fantasy, but the walk to the bus stop was absolutely real. An ounce of nervousness mixed with the excitement swirling around in her head.

She made it just on time, walked on to the half-filled bus, handed her ticket to a stone-faced bus driver and found a seat by the window. She wanted to see every inch of the city as they drove into it. An older woman with a lap full of knitting sat next to her and smiled. The familiarity calmed her a bit. Her mother spent the weekends knitting one and purling two after the morning's chores were finished. It would be a few hours before the skyline even came into view and the slow rocking of the bus soon lulled Abby to sleep.

Two or three hours later, she wasn't sure exactly, a particularly large bump in the road jostled Abby awake. The woman next to her was still knitting what now looked like a child-sized sweater. A quick look out the window revealed the view she'd been dreaming of for eighteen years. Abby clutched the small backpack she brought packed full of all her possessions to her chest and gasped. It was exactly like the pictures, but it also wasn't. Nothing could have prepared her for the jagged line of towering buildings that rose up out of the ground in front of her. The old woman chuckled.

"First time in New York City, dear?"

"Is it that obvious? I've always wanted to visit, but this is the first time my parents actually let me on a bus."

"Well, I prefer the quiet of the country now, but I spent a fair amount of my younger years wandering through the city streets. My daughter lives in Manhattan, so when I visit I get live vicariously through her. I can never stay for too long, though. These old bones can't withstand the hustle and bustle like they used to. Stay out all night for me at least once, will you? There's nothing like Times Square once all the tourists have gone back to their hotels."

Abby tried to assure her that she was going to do everything in New York, especially Times Square, but the woman seemed to lose herself in the memory, smiling down at the knitting in her lap. Abby didn't mind the sudden end to their conversation, it only assured her that sometimes just thinking about being in New York City was better than whatever you were actually doing. Her nails dug into the sides of her backpack as she tried to contain her excitement.

Sarah had given Grace all of Abby's bus information: bus number, time of departure and arrival, where it was going to drop her off. She promised to meet her there and help her figure out the subway.

"I can probably do it on my own. She don't have to go out of her way," Abby had said to Sarah, but Sarah said Grace had laughed kindly and told her there was no way she was going to let an Amish teenage girl get lost in New York on her very first day.

"She might end up wandering around Coney Island and I won't have that."

The streets started to narrow as the bus made it's way deeper into the city and closer to their destination. They passed small corner stores with yellow banners marked "Deli Grocery," and pop-up street vendors selling flowers or fruit or both. Abby tried to remember the face of every new person she saw. Everyone was so different here than in her homogeneous Amish community back home and she loved it. Each unique face had a different story behind it. What did the woman without shoes dressed all in tie-dye do all day? What about the old man in a crisp, tailored suit who read a book while he walked? She loved this city and she hadn't even stepped off the bus yet.

At the bus stop, she recognized Grace right away. Not only could she have been Sarah's somehow older twin, but she was also holding a big poster board sign that said, "Welcome to the Big Apple, Little Amish Girl!" Grace must have recognized her, too, because the moment Abby stepped off the bus she sprinted over and wrapped her in a huge hug, dropping the poster into the street.

"You're finally here! Welcome, welcome, welcome! I'm so excited to have someone from back home come visit me. I love it here, but there's something comfortable about that little town, huh? You excited? You ready for your stay at Casa de Grace?"

Abby knew Grace was kind and outgoing from Sarah's descriptions of her, but she had no idea how energetic she was. Going from the quiet, slow-talking lifestyle back home to Grace's immediate exuberance matched only by the city's chatter behind her was a little overwhelming for her. She could only manage an enthusiastic smile and nod while stumbling over the words, "Yes, okay, I'm ready!" Grace released her from the hug, picked up her sign with one hand, and locked hands with Abby with the other. Abby watched Grace's free-flowing curly hair bounce along behind her as she chatted about everything she wanted to do together while Abby was here. She had dyed it red and let it loose after moving to the city, and Abby admired it. Her dusty blonde locks were almost always pinned tightly to the back of her head and hidden under a bonnet. She left the bonnet at home this time, but the pins remained. She wondered if Grace would help her dye her own hair, maybe black, or blue even. Her parents would love that.

Grace excitedly rattled on about Strawberry Fields in Central Park, and eventually making it to the Statue of Liberty because she hasn't been there in ages, and of course they had to see a Broadway show, there were supposed to be a couple good ones premiering soon, never letting go of Abby's hand. A couple of blocks later, they descended into a subway station and stopped at an automated kiosk to purchase a MetroCard. Abby had never interacted with a machine this complex before and almost froze, not quite knowing what to do with the ball of crumpled bills in her hand. Luckily, Grace was quick to remember what life back home was like and thoughtfully helped her through the process. Holding the bright yellow and blue card in her hand made her feel very grown up and independent. She even made it through the turnstile on the first try.

"You're a natural, Abby! You were made for New York," exclaimed Abby.

Maybe I am, Abby thought.

Mama and Papa may have had more to worry about than a daughter with blue hair.

Grace took a break from listing every attraction in New York City to look down at her cell phone as they took their seats. Abby wrapped her arms tightly around the backpack on her lap and looked around the half-filled car. The subway was a completely new experience for her. She had never been on a bus before, either, but she had seen buses and the types of people on them. *This is like, an underground bus,* she told herself, not completely comfortable with being so far beneath the earth. She focused on the other people sharing the car. Just like the people on the street, no two of them were exactly the same. A tattooed mother sat quietly bouncing a child in her lap, while a teen a few seats down mirrored that image with a boom box blaring hip-hop.

Abby jumped as the train began to move. Grace chuckled and put a hand on her arm.

"I did the same thing on my first subway ride. Turned out I was on the right train but headed the wrong way so I had bigger fish to fry than dealing with being on a train for the first time," she threw back her head and laughed at the memory. "Once I realized I was no where near where I wanted to be I got off the train and started asking people which train would take me where I needed to be and they just kept telling me the one I was on. I didn't realize that the train going in the right direction was just on the other side of the platform. Man, did I feel dumb, but you won't have to worry about that, you have me!"

The two girls chatted for a little while as the train made it's way to their stop. Once they emerged back onto the city streets Abby began to get a feel for the constant flow of people. She quickened her pace to match Grace's and only bumped shoulders with a handful of people as she weaved through the crowd. Eventually, they walked into a tall building where a man sat at a desk by the door.

"Morning, Fred! This is my, well, she's basically my cousin. Abby's gonna be staying with me for a while so don't surprised if she comes flying through here at all hours of the day, okay?"

"Not a problem, Gracie! A friend of yours is a friend of mine. Nice to meet you, Abby!"

Abby smiled and waved at him as they walked to the elevator. She was surprised at how friendly everyone seemed to be. On the odd occasion that she did get her parents to talk with her about New York all they had to say about it was how unwholesome and rude the people were. She'd have to tell them how wrong they were when she got back. *If* she went back.

"That's my doorman, Fred. He's awesome. Always happy to see you even in the middle of the night. If you get yourself locked out or something and I'm not around Fred will help you out."

"That's good to know, thanks. Is everyone in New York this friendly?"

Grace laughed again.

"Not at all. Don't get me wrong, you'll find friendly people if you look for them but a lot of people would run you over with their cars and never look back. They're not bad people, they just have things to do and places to be and no time to stop and check if you're alive or not. That's your problem."

Grace saw a look of dismay cross over Abby's face.

"Don't worry, though. I'll make sure to introduce you to all the best people in New York. You just make sure not to get hit by any cars."

The elevator dinged as they made it to the fourteenth floor. Grace's apartment was at the end of the hall. It had two bedrooms, both with views overlooking the busy streets below, a small kitchen, a bathroom to share, and a living room filled with paintings and posters and a million other colorful decorations. Abby noticed a picture of Grace and Sarah from years ago sitting on a table by the couch. Before she could walk over to get a better look, Grace waved her into one of the two bedrooms. The room had a few pieces of art on the walls, but wasn't near as covered as the living room. A small bed was pushed up against the wall and dresser sat across from it with a TV placed on top.

"This is your room! I moved a bunch of stuff out of it and into the living room so you wouldn't be overwhelmed. I've only been here for a couple of years but I've managed to collect so much junk. I guess that's what happens when you go from a simple Amish life on the family farm to the big city. I can show you how to use the TV, too. I wouldn't blame you if you spent your first couple of days here just sitting in front of it watching cartoons. I know I did."

It was tempting, but Abby had been waiting to be a part of this city for so long she almost felt cooped up just being in the room to drop her things off.

"I'll definitely watch some TV later, but right now all I want is to explore or maybe find I job. I promised my parents I wouldn't ask them for money."

"Oh! I forgot to tell you. I know the manager of the diner down the street. He said he was looking for waitresses so I told him about you. He wants you to come down tomorrow morning so he can make sure you're not a total klutz or anything but you've basically got the job! How do you feel about pancakes?"

"I love pancakes! Thank you so much, Grace. You've done too much already."

"Don't even worry about it. I know what it's like being cooped up on a farm with no electricity or entertainment or fun. I want to make sure you're trip is the complete opposite of that! All fun, all the time. So, what do you want to do first?"

They spent the rest of the day just walking around Manhattan. They stopped for coffee at a sidewalk café, bought a few outfits fit for work at a department store, watched the dogs run around at the dog park. It was a fairly average day in New York but to Abby it was the best day of her life. Grace was a wealth of information, only stopping the flow to take sips of her latte. She knew the best place to get a burger, the best place for live music, the best cup of coffee – this wasn't it, but it would do.

"It's almost dinner time so why don't we start with the best Chinese takeout and spend the evening just hanging out at my place. How does that sound? You must be exhausted!"

She was exhausted, but she'd never admit it. She could only agree that Chinese food did sound good, even though she'd never had it before, and she wouldn't mind a night in. They stopped at a hole-in-the-wall restaurant only distinguishable by its vaguely oriental décor. Grace never once looked at the menu as she rattled off a list of food: crab rangoons, fried rice, sweet and sour chicken, lo mien, and don't forget the fortune cookies! When they got back to the apartment, Grace spread the feast out on her coffee table, handed Abby a pair of chopsticks, and said "Dig in!" After some fumbling with the sticks, she was able to shovel mountains of delicious and greasy food into your mouth.

While they watched the movie "Mean Girls," one of Grace's favorites, Abby broke open a fortune cookie. One side listed a handful of lucky numbers and the other said, "A big surprise is coming your way." She had spent so much time planning for this trip, accounting for every little detail, she wondered what surprises the city could possibly have in store for her. She could hardly sleep that night thinking about it. Maybe she wouldn't get the job. Maybe New York wouldn't live up to her expectations, but that couldn't be it because they already had. Maybe it would be something else, something so surprising that she couldn't even imagine it yet. She hoped that was it.

***

In the morning, Grace woke Abby up with a gentle shake and a steaming cup of coffee.

"Morning sunshine! It's your first day of work and I don't want you to be late. Here, I made you some coffee and I picked out an outfit for you last night, but you don't have to wear it. Sorry I'm acting like such a mom after you came all this way to get away from your parents. Yikes!"

Abby laughed, "I wasn't running *away* from my parents, I was running *to* New York! Thank you for the pleasant wakeup call."

"Well, I was definitely running from my parents. Living in that house was stifling; all those rules, no fun, and for what? God's plan? Sorry, I just get a little frustrated sometimes thinking about all the things my parents kept from me back home. I still feel religious from time to time, but the rigid rules of Amish life just aren't for me."

"Yeah, I know what you mean. I feel like there's so much I want to do that I just can't there. That's why I wanted to come here. I want to get it all out of my system so that I can go back to living simply. Once I've done everything I'll probably be so exhausted that I'll want to go back anyways!"

Grace smiled at her kindly, but bit her tongue. She knew better than most that it didn't always work that way. She didn't want to influence Abby's choice either way, but life as she saw it couldn't just be flushed out of someone's system. A person either craves an Amish life, or an English one. Abby just had to decide which it was she wanted most.

"We can talk about the serious stuff later. Why don't you jump in the shower and get ready for work while I cook breakfast. Go ahead and use whatever you find in there. Mi shampoo es tu shampoo!"

Abby washed herself, changed into the clothes Grace picked out for her, and played around with her makeup. Back home she didn't have any of this stuff. You didn't need makeup to go to church. Plus, every boy she knew had known her since they were children. They'd just be confused if she showed up to the Sunday sing one day covered in powders and creams, but here, no one knew her. She could wear as much or as little makeup as she wanted and no one would question it. Abby decided to start small, only applying a small amount of blush and a couple coats of mascara. The thick frame of lashes made her eyes look huge and the soft pink on her cheeks gave her the appearance of being a little bit warm. Even this small amount of makeup looked jarring in the mirror, but she also kind of liked it.

When she finally emerged from the bathroom Grace was dancing around her kitchen using a spatula as a microphone. At the end of an exaggerated spin she saw Abby standing in the hall giggling.

"Hey! You look awesome! You even threw on some makeup? That's advance level stuff. Now you just need to learn to flirt a little bit and you'll be swimming in tips."

"I know how to flirt!" Abby said defensively.

"Ha! Staring at a boy across the room during prayer is not flirting. New York's a completely different world."

"Oh yeah? How different can city boys be?"

"You know what? You might be right. All you have to do is blink those big doe eyes at one of these too-cool-for-school guys and they'll be smitten. You'll do fine."

"I don't even know if I want to date anyways."

"Oh, you'll change your mind the first time a cute boy tells you he likes your smile. Trust me. It happens to the best of us."

They talked a little bit about boys and back home over breakfast before it was time for Abby to head to the diner. It was so close to Grace's apartment building that she brought Abby down to the lobby, pointed to the place on the corner, sent her on her way and told her to ask for a man named Greg. She was a little nervous to go on her own, but this was exactly the experience that she was hoping to have in New York. Abby craved a taste of independence and she was finally getting it.

The diner was called "Rizzo's Place" and it looked exactly how she'd pictured a classic New York diner. The tables and chairs were all covered in turquoise vinyl complete with little flecks of glitter and the wait staff were all wearing crisp white aprons and matching paper hats. The aprons reminded her of her mother's back home, but that was the only ounce of familiarity she felt. The restaurant was fairly busy. Early morning was their rush hour, but that had passed so only a handful of stragglers and early lunch-eaters remained. She was standing by the doorway when a man only a little older than her wandered over to see if she wanted a table.

"Hey there! Can I help you?"

"I'm looking for Greg. I'm supposed to start working today."

The man's face broke out into a huge smile and he leaned in for a hug.

"You must be Abby! Grace told me all about you and how hardworking and great you are. Grace and I are like this," he crossed his fingers to show that they were close, "so I'd do anything for that girl. Oh! I'm Greg by the way."

Abby gathered from his tone that he might be gay. She had met one gay boy before back in her town, but he hadn't told anyone aside from her and a few friends about his sexuality. It wasn't something that bothered her, but seeing a man so openly flamboyant surprised and encouraged her. She had always thought of New York as a place where everyone could be exactly who they wanted to be, and seeing this man live up to that ideal was exciting. Abby smiled back and nodded.

"That's me! Thank you so much for giving me this job."

"You're so cute! Abby, you're going to fit in just fine here. I almost don't even think I have to train you. Want to just throw on an apron and dive right in?"

When a nervous look crossed over Abby's face he added, "All you have to do first is introduce yourself and ask if they'd like anything to drink. They usually just want coffee or water. If they want coffee make sure to ask about cream and sugar. I'll only give you one table for now so don't worry! If you flop, I'll be here to help you out but you seem like a natural!"

Greg scoped the restaurant to see which table he wanted to throw at her.

"Okay, there's one guy sitting in the corner. He's a regular. He usually just comes in for a coffee, sometimes scrambled eggs with a side of bacon, but nothing too complicated. Nice guy. Are you ready?"

Abby nodded. Greg smiled and gently pushed her forward. She didn't realize how quickly she'd be thrown into the actual serving part of the job, but she wasn't about to embarrass herself so she threw back her shoulders and approached the table as confidently as she could.

"Hey there! I'm Abby. Can I get you a coffee to drink? I mean, can I get you anything?"

From far away she couldn't tell how subtly attractive the man in the booth was. He was partially hidden by a beanie hat and an oversize sweatshirt, but when she got closer Abby could see a sharp jaw line and kind eyes beneath the baggy outerwear. She was thrown off by her attraction for a moment, but her desire to impress her new boss prevailed. She flashed him a professional smile as she bit her tongue.

"Yeah, sure, a black coffee would be great."

"Can I get you anything else?"

"Not right now, thanks."

She turned on her heal and walked back to Greg, not sure where she was supposed to take the order. Luckily, he was watching enthusiastically from the sidelines cheering her on silently.

"How'd it go? Was he nice? What am I saying, he's always nice! What did he order?'"

"Just a black coffee."

"Yep, that sounds like him. Let me show you where the coffee station is."

Greg helped her find the station and pour a cup. He showed her where the cream and sugar was, just in case her next customer needed it. He then showed her how to use the computer system in order to keep track of what each customer ordered. This was all very simple, however, and it wasn't long until she was right back at her only customer's table with the cup of coffee.

"Here you are, sir. One cup of black coffee."

"Thanks, but why are you talking like that. It sounds like you're a robot who was programmed to work in a diner."

Abby blushed.

"Oh, well it's my first day. Sorry. I'm still trying to get the hang of things."

The customer looked a little embarrassed as well. He didn't mean to call her out.

"No, I mean, I'm sorry. I didn't mean to embarrass you. Thanks for the coffee. It's great, as always."

Abby gave him a polite, but uncomfortable, half smile and turned to walk away but he stopped her.

"Wait, what's your name?"

"Abby."

"Abby, like Abigail?"

"No. Just Abby, actually. My mom just liked Abby."

"That's a nice name. Mine's Mac, like Mackenzie. My mom wanted a girl, but got me instead, so she picked a gender-neutral name. I don't mind it, though."

"I like Mac. There aren't a lot of guys where I'm from with names like that."

"Oh yeah? Where is it that you're from?"

"It's a little Amish town just outside of here, actually. I just got into the city yesterday."

"Yesterday? You need someone to show you around then."

Abby blushed again. She thought about what Grace said about flirting for tips, but this felt more genuine than that. This guy, Mac, didn't seem to care about tips.

"I'd like that."

"Great! Give me your phone number and I'll call you up sometime."

"Oh, I don't have a phone number. I don't have a phone."

"That's right. The whole 'Amish' thing. Well, when do you get off here?"

Greg had been listening in the whole time and jumped into the conversation.

"Right now! She's done for the day, wasn't she amazing? I just have to teach her how to clock out and she'll be on her way!"

Greg pulled Abby to the side to chat, but Abby was confused.

"Did I do something wrong? Do you not want me to work here?"

"No! No, of course not. I've just seen this guy come in day in, day out and, don't get me wrong he's one of the nicest customers we have which is why I'm doing this, but he's never once brought in a date or left with one. It's just so cute seeing you two together I can't resist! Go! Have a good time and come back tomorrow and we'll give you some real training. It was my mistake for giving you the cute, single guy as your first table."

Abby almost didn't know what to do. She expected to start her first job, but instead she was going on her first date. She walked back over to Mac's table, Greg casually waving his hands to encourage her.

"Sorry about that. It looks like I'm free now."

"Great! I can take you to work with me then."

Abby had no idea what this entailed but Greg gave her a thumbs up and she followed Mac out of the diner. They walked for a few blocks, casually chatting about their lives. Mac was very interested in Abby's Amish community and Abby was very interested in where Mac was taking her. If it hadn't been for Greg's insistence, she probably wouldn't have felt comfortable following a man she just met through New York City, but she couldn't resist. Eventually, he led them into a building and up a few flights of stairs. Greg pulled back a sliding iron door to reveal a colorful studio filled with paintings and sculptures.

"This is where I work, and live, I guess."

"You're an artist!" Abby exclaimed.

"I'd like to think so, but I've been in a rut lately. I haven't been able to create anything new. I don't want to sound cliché, but would you mind if I tried painting you? You haven't even taken off your work apron yet and your eyes are just so beautiful."

He didn't comment on her smile, but Grace's words still ran through her mind as this boy asked if she'd model for him. On one hand, she was weary, but on the other his sincerity penetrated through most else. She didn't feel as though he wanted anything from her except for her image so she agreed. Mac and Abby sat mostly still for the next couple of hours as Mac swept acrylics across a large canvas, capturing Abby in that moment. When the painting was finally done he turned it around and approached her.

"Alright, here it is. How do you like it?"

Abby looked at herself, carefully depicted in paint. Mac had noticed her mascara covered eyes, but hadn't painted them in a cartoonish way. He'd only enhanced the features on her face that had already been beautiful.

"It's...gorgeous! Is that conceded to say?"

"No, not when you look like you do."

Mac leaned towards Abby to kiss her. She almost turned away, but her instincts took over. With his mouth on hers she finally felt free of her parents grasp and also just free in general. He pulled away before she was finished enjoying the moment.

"I don't want to overstep my boundaries here. I like you a lot, but where from two different worlds."

Abby smiled confidently for the first time and touched his face.

"This is exactly what I want," she said before leaning back in to finish the kiss.

***

The two teens dated for a few weeks after that first studio session. Abby posed for multiple paintings, some more revealing than others, but always with her expressed consent. She loved having her freedom. She loved being able to come and go from Grace's apartment as she wished, but eventually she got bored. One night, as Mac painted Abby holding a bouquet of roses while sitting on a couch, she finally hit her breaking point. She threw the roses up into the air and started to shout.

"Mac! I can't do this anymore. What's the point of me coming here, day after day, just to be your model?"

"You're gorgeous, Abby. You're my muse!"

"But what am I getting out of this? Where does this take me?"

Mac couldn't answer that and Abby got up to leave.

"This has been fun, Mac, but I don't have a purpose here. I think I need to go home."

Mac tried to convince her to stay. He tried to convince her that her portraits meant more to him than just simple trinkets, but she wasn't swayed. As fun as the city was, as much freedom as she had, home would always be back in her little farm town. God had always had a path laid out for her, and this turned out to be only a detour.

AMISH ANGELS

NANCY MANN

"Father, please don't –!"

The plea came too late and was unheeded as a bucket of cold water was released onto Emilia's head, about her bonnet and down along the front of her dress.

"Father!" she screamed, furiously. "Why on earth would you do such a thing!"

Jumping from her chair, she whirled around to face him, her brown eyes flashing with anger. To her dismay, he was beaming as if he had bestowed some act of kindness upon her.

"Emilia, it is summertime! You are cooped up within the walls of a house, knitting a sweater," he replied, reaching out to take her arm. "I do believe that the sunshine is calling your name."

"A sweater that is now ruined!" Emilia complained but allowed for Abel to lead her from the dark stone house into the yard, dripping water heavily along the way. Her two younger sisters were engaged in a game of hopscotch on the road, their long braids flailing in the wind.

"You see? Even the children know better than to stay indoors when the day is fraught with beauty. What kind of example are you setting for the young ones?"

"Father, I do not have time for trivial tasks. I needed to have that sweater finished for the marketplace. After which I have to begin making supper. Now I will be up half the night knitting!"

"Ah! One less sweater at the marketplace will not be the end of days. Also, you do not have to make supper tonight. We have been invited to the home of our neighbor." Emilia turned and looked at him suspiciously at the sudden announcement.

"Which neighbor?" she demanded. Again, Abel smiled, undaunted by his eldest daughter's scrutiny.

"The new members of our community. They reside only a few houses down the road."

"Father, you don't mean that sour faced man with the sullen little girl, do you? I did not like the looks of those two at church. They seem to not like being here. We don't know anything about them."

"My dear, you do not like the look of anyone. That is because you don't truly look at anyone. And that is why we are going this evening; to learn about them and make them feel welcome. "

"Oh father, that is simply not accurate. I do not engage in silliness like other women. I much prefer my own company to idle chit chat. There is no harm in that. I believe it shows that I have a strong head on my shoulders."

"Indeed, it does, my daughter. Once in a while, however, you can relax and enjoy the sunshine." Emilia did not reply. This was an old argument. Since the passing of her mother six years earlier, Abel Troyer had done his best to keep his three daughters in high spirits. The two youngest had eventually moved on from the unexpected death but Emilia had clung to the memory of her mother like a spider web shawl, refusing to let light into her life. Abel desperately missed the infectious sound of Emilia's laughter, a tone which used to ring through the hills of their community like a tinkling bell.

"Regardless, father, I see no reason why we should join Mr. Bawell and his daughter for supper," Emilia finally said. "But if you feel you must, by all means, do go without me."

"It is my wish that we attend supper at their residence and so we shall. I am still the head of this household, Emilia. I do not appreciate being contradicted." Abel was beginning to lose his good humor. He did not understand why everything had to be a fight with Emilia. When his wife had been alive, Emilia had been the model child, obedient and respectful. He knew she only wanted to be left alone to her brooding but he would not have it. She was perfectly healthy, a lovely, kind hearted woman who deserved happiness. It was his job as her father to ensure that she received it. Emilia wisely closed her mouth and turned to face her siblings as her father walked off into the back part of the yard, seeming to have no more interest in teasing his child.

"Emmy, will you play with us?" Collette called, her blonde hair almost white in the droplets of sunlight. Emilia forced herself to smile and shook her head. For a fleeting moment, she was tempted to join the children but she pushed the thought from her mind.

"Not today, Collette. I have work to do."

"You always have work to do, Emmy!" Evelyn pouted. Collette took her younger sister's hand and pulled the nine-year-old toward the veranda.

"She is busy taking care of us, Evie. We are going to mammi and dawdy's now anyway. We must get dressed."

"Wait one moment, Collette. You're going to mammi and dawdy's house? Father just said that we are going to our new neighbor's for supper. Are you certain?"

Collette paused at the door to allow Evelyn to pass.

"You and papa are going to Aaron Bawell's for supper. Evie and I are going to mammi and dawdy's." The girls disappeared into the house and Emilia was left on the porch, still dripping from her father's cold water bath. She narrowed her smoky eyes. *Why is he sending Evie and Collette to our grandparents' house? What is papa up to?* She cringed inwardly as she had her suspicions.

"Emilia, why do you insist on being so stubborn?"

"What is it, father? What have I done now?"

Abel sighed heavily and stared at his daughter as she descended the stairs from her bedroom.

"You know full well that you cannot attend this supper wearing working clothes. Please change into more appropriate attire." Emilia blinked her solemn eyes at him.

"But father, I believed this to be work." Abel scowled and pointed firmly up the staircase.

"You will do as I say immediately, Emilia. And that is quite enough of your impudence for one day." Emilia hung her head in shame, immediately reading her father's anger and slightly stung by his words. Abel was not one to raise his voice in anger.

"Yes father. I'm sorry." She hurried back up to change her clothes and wondered why she had performed such a defiant act. She knew that her father would not have allowed her to visit the Bawell house dressed in rags. It was disrespectful. Lately she had been feeling more and more feisty and if she was not already well into her late twenties, she would have thought that she was due to experience rumspringa. She had briefly experimented with cigarettes and beer when she was younger but she had since been baptized and was very happy in the community. Well, as happy as Emilia could be. There was an unsurmountable void which had filled Emilia since the death of her young mother. She was eternally grateful for the consistency and love given by Abel, however, Emilia and her mother had a bond that seemed to outlive death. Time did not heal her pain and eventually Emilia had succumbed to the fact that she was destined to be discontent for the remainder of her life. Yet lately, the sorrow had turned into some sort of boiling anger and no matter how Emilia tried, she could not seem to tame the beast which was growing within her.

Moments later, she was descending the stairs in a freshly ironed dark blue dress, a starch white bonnet covering her thick head of hair. Abel beamed happily.

"You look lovely. Much better. Shall we?" He offered his arm to his daughter and they started out the door.

"Father, why have you sent the children to mammi and dawdy's this evening?"

"Ah because this evening is for the older people, my dear daughter." Emilia swallowed a knowing grunt but said nothing. As they strolled up the walkway toward the Bawell household, the front door flew open and Emilia was facing the petulant stare of a six-year-old child. Her blue eyes looked like frosted panes of glass as she took in the sight of the two strangers on the porch.

"Good evening, Amity," Abel boomed amiably. "How are you this fine night?"

The girl did not respond and instead turned and disappeared out of view. Emilia gave her father a look but the older man did not meet her eyes. A moment later, Aaron Bawell appeared at the door.

"Please, come in," he said, extending the front door for them to enter. Abel smiled and nodding his thanks while Emilia reluctantly followed.

"May I introduce my daughter, Emilia?" Abel said, removing hat and gesturing toward Emilia.

"Yes," Aaron replied nodding and closing the door. Emilia was slightly taken aback by his disinterested response. In her grief, Emilia had not been interested in the prospect of marriage despite her father's endless prompting.

"It is not healthy for a woman to go through life without a companion, Emilia," Abel had told her countless times. "What of children?"

"I have two daughters in Evelyn and Collette," she had replied, only half jokingly. She had not the stomach to think of child bearing when her own mother had not had the chance to watch her daughters grow up. Eventually, Abel had forsaken the quest to marry off his oldest daughter. However, she had more callers than anyone else in her community and the reason for that was simple. She was the ideal wife. She was hard working, compassionate and a deep thinker. She possessed patience and everyone was a friend to her. Also, she was incredibly lovely, with long honey blonde hair and wide, innocent brown eyes, framed in long eyelashes. Whenever Emilia flashed an elusive smile, the entire world seemed to follow her lead. Even after years of rejecting suitor after suitor, they still came knocking on her door, eager to see her wed to them.

This is why Aaron Bawell's abrupt greeting was so stunning to Emilia. He was apparently unimpressed by Emilia's presence. *He does not know you,* Emilia reasoned, following the men into the sitting room. *He has only been in our district for two weeks. He has no reason to give you a second look.* Even as Emilia thought the words, she felt a strange pang of longing. She oddly wished him to look at her again. And again. *You must stop thinking this way!* She chided herself. *Your thoughts are that of a child in puppy love!* But Emilia could not stop staring at the newcomer and taking in all the details of his strong physique. His voice was deep and mellifluous and Emilia thought she could listen to him speak all day long. She felt a blush color her cheeks and she wondered what it was about Aaron which set him apart from the others who had bid for her hand in marriage. Certainly he was handsome but many men could claim the same. He donned a beard, an indication that he was married but there had been no mention of a mother for his young daughter. Emilia suddenly realized that she was very interested in learning more about the man in whose house she sat. Aaron and Abel were having a conversation of which Emilia heard none. As they finished speaking, Aaron looked about the room, somewhat confused.

"Amity!" Aaron called out. "Join us, please."

His demand was met with no response and sighing heavily after a moment, Aaron rose to his feet.

"Excuse me," he apologized before disappearing into the home. Emilia listened as his footsteps ascended up the staircase.

"Father, what on earth are we doing here?" Emilia asked, feeling distinctly uncomfortable. Abel gave her a sidelong look and smiled briefly.

"I believe you know what we are doing her, Emilia. Aaron Bawell is a successful carpenter. He is new to the community and has not been swayed by your endless rejection. He will be a perfect match for you."

"Father!" Emilia groaned. "I had hoped you had stopped with this matchmaking foolishness long ago."

"Emilia, it is not foolishness to want your children to be happy and begin a family. You are not going to be a young woman forever, child. You must consider your future."

"Father, I – "her words were cut short as Aaron returned to the sitting room, almost dragging along his daughter.

"Papa, I don't want them to be here," Amity Bawell snarled, glaring viciously at the strangers in her living room. Against the flickering kerosene lanterns, she almost looked diabolical, her small upper lip curled above her teeth, blue eyes aflame. She was otherwise a very pretty child, a spitting image of her father. She had long, straight black hair and cornflower blue eyes. Her features were softer, less defined than Aaron with his high cheekbones but she also had the extra fat of a small child.

"You will mind your manners!" Aaron snapped back, shooting an embarrassed look toward Abel.

"I do not like you!" Amity yelled, hands on her hips, addressing Emilia. Emilia was shocked by the defiance in the girl. She could not imagine either of her sisters ever speaking in such a way. *I don't believe I am overly fond of you either, little devil,* Emilia thought, narrowing her eyes at the child.

"Amity! You will stop this insolence immediately!" Aaron thundered, rising to his feet once more. "We are in the presence of guests. Your mother would be ashamed of your behavior!"

As if her father had physically struck her, Amity seemed to crumble to the floor. Her face went waxen and her eyes filled with tears. The deviousness evaporated and suddenly Emilia was staring at an ashen faced child. For a moment, she felt her heart crack. She had never seen a sorrier sight. Amity opened her mouth as if she were about to speak but no words fluttered from her small, pink lips. Then, tears streaked her chubby face and she ran, sobbing, from the room. Heavily,

Aaron reclaimed his seat beside Abel. There was an awkward silence as everyone searched for the right words to speak. Finally, Abel cleared his throat, standing.

"We will call another time, Aaron," Emilia's father said magnanimously, ushering Emilia to her feet. "Young girls can have their bad days. I understand. I have three of them."

Abel put a smile to his statement to ease the younger man's discomfort but Aaron looked devastated, his deep blue eyes troubled and full.

"Every day is a bad day." He seemed to have heard the way his words sounded and he quickly rose to his feet.

"I apologize. I thought we had been here long enough for her to accept visitors. This transition has been extremely difficult on Amity." Aaron looked imploringly at Abel for understanding, completely ignoring Emilia. Inwardly she was shaking her head. *You are far too soft on the child. You should not make excuses,* Emilia thought. *These people are not the right fit for this community. We do not rear our children to act so recklessly.*

"Of course it has! She is but a small girl. She cannot be expected to understand so much change in so little time," Abel assured him. "Give her time."

"I will speak to the Bishop about her," Aaron promised, ushering them toward the door. "Once more, please forgive this disruption. I will reschedule our meal for another time."

"Please, do not worry. Perhaps next time you will visit with us. Evelyn is only a few years older than Amity. A friend may do her a world of good." Aaron looked thoughtful at the suggestion and nodded. The men bid each other adieu and Aaron closed the door in their wake without so much as a glance at Emilia. Again, she was stunned by his rudeness. Abel took Emilia's arm and guided her down the path leading to their modest house moments down the road. When she was quite sure they were out of earshot, Emilia turned to her father.

"Lord above, I have never seen such an ill behaved child in all of my life!" she exploded. "And that man, he's rude – "

"Emilia – "Abel attempted to cut her off but she was not finished.

"He barely spoke one full word to me. I see that the apple does not fall far from the tree! Can you imagine raising a child so willful – "

"Emilia – "

"And you, you father, why on God's green earth would you ever consider him a match for me?"

"Are you quite finished with your diatribe?" Abel asked tiredly, releasing her arm as they approached their house.

"You can't say that you weren't shocked at her behavior, father," Emilia said, baffled by his calm demeanor.

"I was not," Abel replied. Emilia arched an eyebrow, her brown eyes cynical.

"How not?"

"I was not surprised because you and your sisters behaved very similarly after your mother passed also." A wave of dizziness overwhelmed Emilia as his words set in, instantly followed by deep regret.

"You mean to tell me that Amity's mother has recently passed away?" she whispered.

"Yes. Not three weeks ago. That is why Aaron has uprooted his life and started fresh here. Amity could not bear to be in their home without her mother. He is doing his best for his daughter. You could stand to be more empathetic, daughter. You know better than anyone how difficult a time this is for someone in their position."

Emilia paused on the veranda, staring after her father. Slowly, she turned to stare up into the dusky sky. Her heart was heavy with sadness but for the first time since she could remember, the woe she felt was not for herself but for the small girl missing her mother and the man who could not take her pain away.

II

The following morning, Emilia dressed and fed her sisters before delivering them to their school. Their morning chatter was often the highlight of Emilia's day but that dawn, she could not get the sight of Amity Bawell's anguished blue eyes out of her head as if they were etched into her skull. Oh how she understood the poor child's misery and she desperately wished that there was a way to help the girl overcome her fresh loss. Of course, she knew from personal experience that there was no such way. The Bishop would tell her that time, family and community would help expel the pain but Emilia knew that was a lie he would tell everyone. Over and above that, Emilia found her mind traveling to Aaron's Bawell. He was still such a young man to be widowed. Abel had informed her that they had been wed eight years when cancer claimed Aaron's wife, Beth. She had been sickly for a very long while before finally succumbing to her grave. Amity had watched her mother wither away before her eyes and when she finally did go to her final rest, Aaron had immediately acted, taking Amity away from the horrible memories and the house in which her mother had suffered so greatly.

"No child should ever have to see their parent in a state like that," Able had said sadly. "Especially one so young. They cannot begin to reconcile what is happening. In a way, it is a blessing that your mother was take so quickly. She was never in agony which you girls had to witness."

Emilia swallowed the lump in her throat and nodded but she wasn't sure if she agreed. *Maybe mama wasn't in agony but we were. And some of us still are.* Emilia forced herself to think about Aaron and Amity. She vowed that she would befriend the newcomers at once. It would not make their life more bearable but it would help shoulder the burden they were carrying. The Bishop had been right about one thing; community and family did assist the process somewhat.

After sending the children off and promising to pick them up that afternoon, Emilia carefully constructed a basket of wicker and filled it with several thought-filled items. There was a freshly knit blanket she had intended to sell at the market, jars of preserves and honey, a mutton pie and a bouquet of wildflowers. She gently wrapped the basket in another wool blanket and carried the package outside and down the laneway. There was a charged nervousness about her as she knocked on the door to the Bawell house. There was no sign of movement from within the walls but the curtains were drawn. Emilia knocked again but to her disappointment, there was no response. *Ah, well I imagine Amity is in school and Aaron is off at work although Lord knows they should be home in their grief. I will just leave this here. I did not pen a note. Maybe I will run home, write a note and bring it back.* Emilia set the gift down on the small porch and was on her way to retrieve a pen and paper. Suddenly, one of the straps to her bonnet came loose and just before a short wind carried it off, Emilia reached up and snatched it back, her whole body turning. Lowering herself from the balls of her feet, she realized she was facing the Bawell house again. Aaron Bawell was standing at the door, staring at her strangely. He was wearing only a white cotton undershirt and a pair of trousers, his beard unkempt and his feet were bare. Even so, he looked incredibly handsome, his black hair a disheveled mess about his finely lined face. He looked down at the basket on the porch and then back to Emilia. She offered him a timid smile.

"My family sent you some goods to help you along," she called out. Again, his steely blue eyes looked at the package. Without a word, he turned and slammed the door behind him, leaving the present on the dusty deck.

"You must not be offended, daughter. He is grieving," Abel told Emilia when she reiterated what happened.

"I know he is grieving, father but even you have to admit that it was unfathomably rude!" Abel shrugged nonchalantly and took a sip of his tea.

"You must not forsake them in their time of need, Emilia. People often are the most trying during their darkest hour of need. It is God's way of testing you to see if you are capable of maintain humility and patience. Also, Aaron has agreed to come here for supper tomorrow evening." Emilia dropped her parring knife and stared at her father in disbelief.

"Oh father, you must stop beating a dead horse! You cannot believe that a recently widowed man is someone whom is interested in marrying your spinster daughter." Abel looked up sharply at her.

"Firstly, you are not a spinster. Not for the time being, mind you...and secondly, it is not my intention to push marriage upon a devastated man. I am merely suggesting you provide comfort to a man and a child who desperately require a support system. Everything is not sordid and dark, Emilia. You must learn that every cloud had a silver lining. And when you learn that, perhaps you can pass that information along to the Bawells." Contritely, Emilia looked at her hands and then continued peeling potatoes. Secretly she was pleased that Aaron and Amity were coming. She had been unable to stop thinking about the man, despite his brusque nature. *He is a hard man to reach, perhaps due to the circumstances.*

"Yes, father," she replied. "What shall I make for supper tomorrow night?"

"Well apparently anything but mutton," Abel jested lightly.

When Aaron and Amity appeared on the veranda of the Troyer home, something seemed different. Amity was no long sulky and angry. She was very quiet and seemed almost out of touch with what was occurring in her presence. Abel introduced her to Evelyn and Collette but she was as disinterested in the girls as Aaron was in Emilia. The entire grouping was a fiasco and Emilia wanted to escape. As the men and children sipped on lemonade on the porch, Emilia put the finishing touches on supper before calling everyone inside. The men seated at both ends of the table, grace was said and Emilia began to serve generous portions of fried beef cutlets, roasted potatoes and corn. Collette passed bread around the table.

"This is excellent, Emilia. You are a wonderful cook," Abel declared, taking a bite of his meal. She smiled at his transparency and he winked subtly in her direction.

"Thank you, father," she replied. She looked expectantly at Aaron but he continued to eat his food, unspeaking. Emilia felt her heart sink. She was expecting too much from this man. She did not know why she felt so drawn to him, why it was so important that he like her but she could not think of anything she wanted more than for him to look at her and say one kind word. Emilia sighed and put her fork onto her plate, her appetite suddenly depleted. She waited for the others to finish their meal before rising to clear away the dishes. Collette and Evelyn rose to help. When the three siblings were in the kitchen, Collette rolled her dark eyes heavenward.

"What a bore!" she exclaimed.

"Shhh!" Emilia hissed at her sister. "Lower your voice immediately!"

"That girl is odd," Evelyn piped up. "She doesn't say anything!"

Emilia turned and glared at her nine-year-old sister.

"Many people would say you are odd because you say too much! Shame on you both! They are guests in our home and we treat them with the respect they deserve. What's more is you do not ever judge a someone for you do not know where they have come from!" Evelyn looked aghast, completely unaccustomed to being reprimanded by Emilia. Her own limpid eyes filled with tears.

"I didn't mean harm" she whispered. "I'm sorry, Emmy. I respect our guests!"

Emilia was filled with remorse as she watched her sister's face but she stood firm.

"When you respect people, you do not speak ill of them behind their backs. I want you to carefully consider your words before you speak from this day forward. You can cause someone a great deal of harm with your language and imagine how ashamed you will feel if that person needed a friend but instead were only met with idle name calling. You two are better than that! You were raised to be charitable and kind. Do not disappoint papa and I." Nodding, both girls shuffled upstairs to avoid any further punishment. As they disappeared, Abel walked into the kitchen.

"You will make a good mother," he told her quietly.

"Did you hear those two?" Emilia asked, placing a dish towel onto the counter, shaking her head in disbelief, purposely ignoring her father's comment. Abel nodded.

"Yes, I heard them. And I heard what you told them."

"Well it's true. They were raised better than that," Emilia said, reaching into the ice box for the cobbler she had made for dessert.

"I heard something else also," Abel said, drawing closer. Emilia glanced up.

"What else did you hear, father?" Abel gently touched her face so she was looking at him. He smiled genuinely, his eyes twinkling with happiness.

"I heard you call me 'papa.'"

Emilia had just finished hanging the wash on the line when she heard a faint knock at the door. Hurriedly, she picked up the basket and rushed inside. Unceremoniously, she threw open the door and her breath caught in her throat.

"Mr. Bawell!" He had been staring blankly into the yard and seemed to snap out of his reverie when Emilia spoke his name.

"Emilia," he nodded. He had a faraway look in his eye and he bit his lip as if in concentration.

"Are you all right?" Emilia questioned, trying to make sense of why he was standing on the doorstep. Unconsciously, her hand swept through her hair, smoothly the flyaway strands.

"No." Emilia stared expectantly at him, waiting for an elaboration which did not materialize. She sighed. He was still determined to be standoffish and she had far too much to do that day than vie for his affection.

"Mr. Bawell, my father is at the shop if you would like to speak with him," Emilia offered. Aaron blinked at her as if he did not comprehend her words.

"No," he said again, in a flat, monotonous way. "I need you."

Emilia's heart fluttered and she shushed it in her head but a smile could not help but find its way to her lips.

"Oh?" she asked with some uncharacteristic coyness. Her smile faded with his very next words.

"My daughter has vanished. I need you to help me find her."

III

Night had fallen and there was still no trace of young Amity. Aaron Bawell sat perfectly still on a straight back chair, as if his soul had floated away from his body. A search party had formed and they had covered all of the hills and valleys in the district but no one had found a sign of the girl.

"She will turn up. She probably just got lost. They will find her," Abel told Aaron soothingly, trying to force his neighbor to eat and drink but Aaron was unhearing, unseeing and seemingly uncaring. The members of the community gathered in the bishop's home, waiting for word and speculating among themselves.

"Who would abduct a small Amish girl?" they wondered. "Our way is peaceful. This is unheard of!"

"She was not abducted," Emilia suddenly said, an epiphany hitting her full force. There was a murmur of skepticism as she began to pace excitedly, her mind racing.

"How can you know that, Emilia? This is commonplace with the English. Kidnapping and such. A stranger must have wandered off with her."

"No one wandered off with her," Emilia told them. "She has not been kidnapped."

"What do you believe happened to her?"

For the first time in hours, Aaron looked up, his once vacant eyes filled with hope.

"Where is my daughter, Emilia?" he begged, his voice hoarse with emotion.

"She went to where her mother is resting."

Amity had been walking for over seven hours, her little legs exhausted as she trekked toward her old district. It was Aaron himself who had found his small daughter, asleep on the side of the dirt road, completely hidden to eyes not searching. Her cheeks were caked in salted tears, her nose completely blocked from the endless crying her journey had seen. Aaron had flown off the carriage before it had come to a complete halt. He scooped up his daughter in strong arms and held her tightly but even that gesture did not wake the child from the depth of her sleep. Swaddling her like an infant, Aaron carefully placed her in the back of the wagon and sat with her as Abel took the reins and began the journey back to Latham District. Emilia sat in the wagon with father and daughter. Assured that Amity was still asleep, Aaron turned to the lovely blonde across from him. She could not make out his face as the wagon was dark and the night, moonless.

"How did you know?" he finally asked her. "How did you know where she had gone?"

Emilia was silent a moment. Ever since she had learned of Beth's death, it was as if a floodgate of memories had taken Emilia over. She began reliving every painful event which occurred from the moment her own mother had passed. When Aaron had arrived on the doorstep that afternoon, Emilia hadn't immediately made the connection but as time went on, it became clearer that Amity had not been taken and instead had run off somewhere. There was only one place the child wanted to be; with her mother. Of course Emilia knew that. That feeling was still very fresh in her own heart.

"I was Amity not too many years ago," Emilia told Aaron. "I understand how she feels."

There was a deep quiet from the other side of the transportation.

"I tried very hard," Aaron finally said.

"It is not easy," Emilia agreed.

"No. It is worse than that. Beth was sick for a great while. I had expected her to pass from when Amity was two years old. But she was a fighter, our Beth. She would get well and then get sick again, well and sick once more, each time getting worse and worse. Her body was failing. Everyone could see it including Beth. Our entire community knew it was only a matter of time. But Amity was just a baby. She only saw her mother. And she had so much hope that her mother would get well." Again, there was silence. Emilia opened her mouth to speak some words of comfort when Aaron took a breath.

"I despised my wife at the end of her life, Emilia. God help me, it's the truth. I loathed the fact that she would not give up and would continue to put our daughter through the trauma of watching her fall ill time and again. I am a despicable person. What kind of man wants his wife to die?" There was a catch in his voice and Emilia swallowed the lump in her own throat.

"The kind of man who cannot bear to watch others suffer," she answered quietly. "A very noble man. A man who loves his daughter so much that it tore him apart to watch her cry day after day for her mama." *A man like my father,* Emilia thought, her heart swelling with love for the man in the front of the carriage.

"I have been very uncouth to you, Emilia," Aaron suddenly said from the darkness. His voice was gruff.

"You have been grieving," she replied. "I do not consider a grieving man uncouth."

"No. That is not why I have been so uncivilized to you."

Emilia opened her mouth to protest but instead decided to wait for him to continue.

"When Beth found out she was dying, she made me promise to get married immediately so Amity would have a mother. She made numerous suggestions as to who should replace her. I agreed to placate her during her last days but the thought of marrying anyone else, of Amity calling anyone else 'mama' was horrifying and wrong. Some women in my community were overtly suggestive even prior to Beth's passing and when she finally did pass, there were knocks on my door quite literally the next day. That is why I made such a hasty decision to take Amity and leave."

"Ah, you thought I was one of the women vying for position of your wife," Emilia said slowly feeling her face blush crimson. *Oh papa! Do you see what your meddling has done now?*

"No, that's not what I believed, Emilia. I had seen you at church and you were so lovely, my breath actually halted when I laid eyes upon you. I had never felt that way about anyone. You are so beautiful but in a modest, unassuming form. I saw how well everyone has taken to you, how hard you work and how your sisters adore you. You are everything a man could hope for. I knew I had to stay far away from you. Yet when your father approached me in a neighborly fashion, I could not resist inviting you to supper. I wanted you near but I wanted you far away. Do you understand?"

Emilia almost laughed out loud.

"I understand exactly what you mean," she replied. "And now?"

Out of the dark, a large, calloused hand found hers. An unexpected shiver went up her spine at the touch. She squeezed his palm gently.

"And now the thought of marrying anyone other than you is horrifying and wrong." Aaron squeezed her hand back and for the first time since her mother died, Emilia felt the weight of the world lift off her shoulders.

She was actually happy.

END

ALWAYS AMISH

MEGHAN MASON

Sarah's day began as any other. The sky was clear and blue with a scattering of pillow clouds, and Sarah was walking the two mile stretch between her home and her father's general store in town. Each morning she had to arise from her sleep before sunrise to fulfill all the household duties. There were chickens to be fed, produce to be picked, and breakfast to be prepared for herself, her daed, Jacob, and her two younger siblings. Sarah was the oldest, at seventeen, then came her schwester Hope at nine years old, and finally boppli bruder, Noah. Their maam had passed away during childbirth just a year ago next month. Noah had not even had his first birthday yet. In Amish life, this meant that Sarah, being the eldest daughter, was now responsible for keeping house and raising her younger siblings. It was an enormous responsibility, but one that Sarah did with a willing and loving heart. She loved to sing softly to herself as she dressed in her pale blue dress, white apron and bonnet. As she completed all the morning chores, Sarah liked to sing her favorite church hymns. It helped to make the chores go by faster, and always served to put her in a good mood.

Today, as Sarah made her way down the dirt path that led to town, she hummed a little tune, and thought about what a long day it would be for her working at her daed's store. She loved her father, but Jacob Williams was renowned in the small Amish community as a very strict task master. He could certainly be overbearing at times, but Sarah understood how difficult life had become for him since her mamm's death. Jacob had loved his wife, Elizabeth very much. They had married at only sixteen years old, and planned on making a life together as they grew in their love for one another into ripe old age. It was not Gott's will however, and now the Williams family had to adjust to life without mamm. Sarah knew her daed was lonely most times, and that that was what made him so domineering at times. It didn't make things any easier on Sarah, however, and taking care of the home, plus working at the store was exhausting. She did this all without complaint, and thanked Gott for her many blessings. The store sold local goods from the community farmers, and some of the women sewed items of clothing or household linens upon special request. Often, specific Englischers would place orders for tablecloths or various linens, and the ladies who had grown children, thus having extra time on their hands, would take up the task.

Sarah entered the store, and greeted her father in traditional Pennsylvania Dutch, as he was of the Old Order who still adhered strictly to Amish customs, "Guder Mariye, daed," she said cheerfully. As per usual, Jacob eyed his eldest daughter with a certain unfounded suspicion, but returned her morning greeting just the same.

"Sarah, there is much to accomplish today. You can start with sweeping and dusting the shelves, and then take over the accounts book. I need to go to see Farmer Pickens about eggs, since he is late with delivery," he stated. This was bound to be a long day, but if she was left alone in the store for most of the day, she could at least indulge herself in singing. Daed did not approve of Sarah's love of song outside of the religious environment or outside the home, as was the custom of her faith. Nonetheless, Sarah felt it to be a harmless enough past time if she wasn't running around town singing for everyone to hear. Jacob watched her as she retrieved the broom, and then he departed for Farmer Pickens'.

As Sarah swept the already very clean oak floors, she sang a lovely hymn from last Sunday's service. It was called, "The Lord Provides," and she loved it because of the sweet notes and fortifying lyrics. She was alone in the store, and she allowed herself to really sing out. Singing was the thing that made her feel the happiest, and soon enough she was in a world of her own.

Outside, a young man strolled along the road, thinking about how relieved he felt about having made the move to a simpler life in the country. He enjoyed the pristine air, and the beautiful woods, and had a healthy respect for the Amish community. The outlying farms and cottages that were not Amish, coexisted peacefully together, respecting one another's privacy and traditions. The town called Havensville was a perfect place to call home after the disaster he had left behind him in the big city of Pittsburgh. The young man was just eighteen, but mature enough to recognize the dysfunction of his family life. His father's alcoholism had been taking its toll on him and his mother for many years, and she had recently passed away from a lengthy battle with cancer. He tried to care for his father, but he would have none of it, and continued his wayward lifestyle. So, after much thought, he decided to leave school, where he was studying music, and start fresh somewhere new. The young man packed his bags, gathered what meager funds he had saved from after school jobs, and caught the next bus out to the countryside. He stopped short when he saw the quaint wooden store in front of him. It was painted a fresh white with simple blue trim, and had a small garden of wildflowers in the front. There was a cobblestone walkway leading up to the entry, and a hanging sign above the door that read, "William's General Store." Nothing flashy, but it was adorned with a little bluebird in the righthand corner of the square sign. The store looked like something out of a storybook with its flowers and front porch swing. He decided he should go in and stock up on supplies and grocery items since this was his very first day in town. He entered the store, and there he observed a modest, yet beautiful young woman singing her heart out as she dusted the many shelves behind the register. Her back was turned to him, and she had not noticed the bell as he had entered the store.

"Excuse me please, miss?"

Sarah gave a startled jump, as she whipped around. She felt embarrassed that she hadn't heard anyone enter the store, and here she was singing away!

"Oh, my goodness! I'm terribly sorry. I didn't hear you come in, sir," Sarah replied.

"It is not a problem. I quite enjoyed your song. You have a lovely singing voice," the young man said. Sarah blushed crimson at his compliment, as she was shy towards strangers, and she had not seen this young man around the village area,

"How may I help you, Mr....." Sarah inquired.

"I am hardly worthy of the title of Mr., but my name is John Anders, and I have only just arrived here in Havensville this early morning," He replied. Sarah thought him a fine-looking man, around her own age, but wondered why on earth he had come here to live in such a small and isolated place, "Where are you coming from, Mr. Anders? And you are with your family, I presume?"

"No, I am here alone from Pittsburgh. It was time for me to start a new life of my own. This place seemed good enough as any other, I guess," offered John, "and please, call me John, and may I ask your name?"

"Ok, my name is Sarah, and my father owns the store. Alright then, John, what would you like?" Sarah began to list what sundries and groceries the simple store offered, but John stopped her, and said he was here for basic living supplies, like food and a few other items such as general toiletries,

"Miss Sarah, I guess I would be grateful if you just took charge and filled my basket with whatever cooking things you think best, and I'll go in search of my personal items?" said John hopefully, as he was not at all knowledgeable about what exactly he would need.

As Sarah made up a large basket of fruits, vegetables, and other things she thought necessary for a young bachelor, John returned to the counter with another basket filled with such items as a hairbrush, toothbrush, toothpaste, sponges, and other assorted things. John thought Sarah was delightful, friendly and kind, and decided to ask her a few questions about Havensville,

"Sarah, thank you for helping me sort out all these things! You are such a help, because this is honestly the first time I have ever been out on my own, and I haven't the slightest clue what I'm planning to do. I do not even have anywhere to stay yet, or any prospects of a job. Do you happen to know of anywhere that may offer a room, and perhaps some honest work?"

Sarah studied John, and figured since he had a gentle looking face and good manners, that she really should help welcome the new comer to his new home. She thought hard for a moment or two, and then replied,

"I know Farmer Pickens has been late with his egg deliveries lately, now that his Betty has had their boppli, oh! I mean baby..." she stammered, remembering that John was likely unfamiliar with their ways of speaking, but without skipping a beat, John said,

"No, please Sarah, use your traditional words. I took the liberty of reading up on Amish tradition and life during the bus ride. I am proud to say that I think I now am familiar with many unfamiliar words!" Sarah was surprised at John's eagerness and willingness to learn some Pennsylvania Dutch, and this only made him more attractive in her eyes.

"Anyways, John, I was going to say that Farmer Pickens might have some dairy work for you, and my daed may like to have a helper with building the new barn at home. He's out at Pickens place, now, but should be returning within the hour," Sarah volunteered. For am Englischer, John Anders was certainly a nice young man, and she was impressed with his independence and desire to fit into the small community.

John smiled, as he paid for his groceries, while Sarah bagged them in plain paper sacks. He was going to have his hands full with these many bags, but he could make it to wherever he was going just fine. He just had to figure out just where it was he was going, and he decided to engage Sarah in more conversation, "Well, perhaps I should wait outside then for your father to return, so that I can sort out some work. I have nowhere in particular to go just now, so I guess your front porch swing is as good a place as any to pass the time." His simple manner made Sarah smile again, and she said he was welcome to the swing while she finished up her duties inside.

"Perhaps you would care for some homemade lemonade when I am finished?" Sarah offered.

"Yes, that sounds wonderful, Sarah. Thank you, kindly! Will you join me then, once you're finished?" he asked hopefully. Again, Sarah blushed, but she did agree to sit awhile on the swing until her father returned, if no other customer came calling. John went outside, and Sarah hurriedly went back to her dusting.

Once outside, John scanned the pretty little porch, and sat down on the swing. It was of fine craftsmanship, and constructed from a sturdy pine, he thought. He sat there quietly thinking that he had made an excellent choice in coming to this place. If everyone was as nice as Sarah Williams, then he was sure to feel at home. Now he just had to find a place to live. He felt a bit nervous, since it was approaching afternoon, and he did not want to be homeless on his first night in a new town. As John was busy fretting about what to do next, Sarah had finished her work, and was preparing a tray of iced cold lemonade. She thought he might be hungry after his long bus journey, and so she made up a plate of sandwiches and sliced some fresh peaches from her own orchard. She had brought them as part of her own midday meal, but felt it would be nice to share with John. She liked the idea of sitting out front with the young man, even though father would probably not approve of her sitting alone with a stranger. She carried the tray outside, and noticed the look of obvious concern on John's face.

"Whatever is the matter, John?" as she placed the lunch things on the side table. John looked thankfully at her, and said,

"Sarah, you certainly did not have to go to such trouble on my account! Thank you. I do feel hungry. To tell you the truth, I am concerned about where I might find lodging for tonight. I am sure I can find something more permanent as I become more familiar with the folks in town," John confided.

"Don't you worry just yet," she reassured him, and poured him a nice glass of lemonade. She placed a sandwich in his lap, and began to make pleasant conversation about the weather, and who was who in town, and so on...John couldn't help but recall her beautiful singing voice when he had first entered the store. She had such a lovely voice! He could think of nothing more wonderful than to hear her singing again, as he missed his music studies, and was a decent singer himself, but he knew he must not seem to forward. He hoped he might someday hear her angelic voice again, as he got to know her better, and realized he was lost in his daydreams of her, as she chattered on. He forced himself back to reality, and listened to everything she was saying regarding life in and around the town. The care she had taken making him sandwiches and sharing the juicy peaches did not go unnoticed. He could not have wished for a lovelier welcome.

Just after a half hour or so, Jacob's horse drawn buggy was making its way towards the store front. Sarah could already see his tense looking eyes, and frowny expression, as he noted that his daughter was sitting unattended with a strange young newcomer. He parked the buggy hastily, and walked briskly up the front steps to the swing,

"What have we here, Sarah? Why are you not minding the store?" he demanded.

"Daed, please welcome Mr. John Anders from Pittsburgh. He has travelled here by bus to make a life for himself, and came in to purchase his necessities," announced his daughter. Jacob stared at the young Englischer with some uneasiness, as he was always wary of outsiders. You never knew how they would take to the Amish customs, after all. Nonetheless, Jacob was not to be a rude man, so he extended his hand in greeting,

"Kannscht du Pennsilfaanisch Deitsch schetzer?" blurted Jacob, knowing full well that Mr. Anders certainly did not speak Pennsylvania Dutch. It was Jacob's way of distancing himself from the young stranger, and he was obviously annoyed that Sarah had engaged him in conversation, and then apparently fed him as well! A little too welcoming, he thought to himself.

"Uh, no, I think what you said was 'Do I speak Pennsylvania Dutch? I confess I am not very familiar with it as of yet, but did have a chance to study some on my way here. I am a quick study, luckily, and hope to pick up the language here and there," John returned quickly. He could understand a father's protective nature, and realized he was the new person in town, so he had better do his best to make a proper first impression,

"It is good to meet you, Mr. Williams," said John, and then Sarah thankfully took over and explained that he was in search of some steady work, and a place to cover his head.

Jacob's predictable answer to this announcement was, "Englischers! Sie scheie sich vun haddiArewat." John made out at least some of what was said, and promptly and wisely replied, "No sir, I am a hard worker, and am willing to take on anything that is available. I need to learn to make my own way in the world now that I am my own man. I can assure you I am a man of my word, and an honest worker for anyone who needs help. I studied music, but am not afraid of a man's work in the fields or building. Whatever needs to be done, I will do it, and I will do it well," promised John Anders. Jacob had to admit that he approved of the boy's answer, though he was no boy, but rather a young man of about eighteen to twenty years of age. As much as he would have preferred otherwise, Jacob knew he needed help building the barn that was to house the new horses, goats, and cows. They were due in for delivery from the neighboring town of Lancaster in three weeks' time, and he would never finish the job alone,

"Tell you what, young Mr. Anders. I need a strong young man to build my barn with me. I'll need ya to be schmaert (smart) and no schlofkopp (sleepyhead)! I'll give ya board in the shack out back. Sarah will make it home for ya, and put some extra furnishings in there. It'll be small, but I imagine it's a darn sight better than nothing.," and as

Jacob had finished his little speech and offer of work and board, John couldn't help but smile wide! This was just perfect, and exactly what he needed, which was not much. Just somewhere to call home, and a place where he could lay his head at night after a hard day's work, "Many thanks, sir! I am much obliged to you for your kind and generous offer." Sarah could only stare blankly at her father's unexpected good nature, and she couldn't help but feel a surge of excitement that John, whom she now considered a friend, would be staying right there on their farm! It would no doubt mean one more mouth to cook and clean for, but she was happy to have the friendly John join her little clan. She enjoyed her household duties, and one more surely would not be any bother.

Jacob said, "Mr. Anders, you wait here till closing time, and we'll go home in the buggy, and get you situated. Sarah, you will have extra work tonight getting Mr. Anders settled and preparing the meal. I expect a satisfying meal, so go on home and get started early then! No time to be standing around on the porch making idle talk," and so he dismissed Sarah, and off she went back home to give that shack a thorough cleaning. By now, Hope would be home from her book learning, and together they could muster what strength they had, and drag some extra furnishings into John's new home. It would take some effort to make that old shack into a home, but she would do it happily for John.

As evening fell, Sarah and Hope had just put the finishing touches on John's new abode, when the buggy arrived. The two men got out, and she noticed that John had not cases or trunk. That meant he had only the clothes on his back! She would start to sewing him some pants and shirts just as soon as she could. But now, there was a beef stew to get on the table for supper, and children to wash up. She practically ran back to the house to check on her stew, and slice the bread. Her father would want dinner on the table straight away.

"Welcome to our home," said Sarah, and she introduced him to each member of the family, including boppli, Noah, and then served up the stew. Everyone enjoyed pleasant conversation, though Jacob kept fairly quiet. He was not one for conversation. Sarah noticed that John ate his supper and hoped that he had had enough to eat. She offered homemade apple tart for dessert, "Sarah, I must thank you for your family's hospitality. I must admit I heard you singing earlier this afternoon in the store! You have an exceptional voice, if you don't mind my saying so. Do you sing at church service? You should not deprive the rest of the town of such a heavenly sound. Do you think you'll sing at the Town Square Picnic your father was telling me about on the way home?" Jacob let his fork drop with a clatter, and John suspected he had somehow misspoke,

"I will have you know, Mr. Anders, that we Amish do not sing for personal glory. Sarah will sing at service only; do you hear that maedel!" spat her father. Sarah already knew how her father felt about her love for singing, and couldn't help but feel sorry for the way John must feel at her father's reproach. Sarah nodded in agreement, and quietly resumed eating her apple tart. When dinner was finished, she cleared the table, and washed up the dishes. Meanwhile, Jacob had taken John out to survey the barn building, and explain what was needed in the coming three weeks. It was going to be a stretch, thought John, to get that barn built in time for the animals, but a promise was a promise. He'd get the job done mostly on his own while Jacob was working at the store. Then they would work on it together till dark in the weeks to come.

John made his way to his meager home, but upon entering the front door, he was amazed at what a spectacular job Sarah had done sprucing the place up! The wooden floors gleamed and smelled like fresh soap, and she had put pretty little curtains up around the window. He felt badly that she had been put to such trouble dragging in furniture, but was relieved to see it was just a simple chair and table, a cot made up into a comfy looking bed. She had supplied him with lots of fluffy blankets and a pillow, and there was a plain white porcelain ewer and basin for washing. It was perfect! Simple and comfortable was all he wanted or needed. He felt a strange stirring in his heart that Sarah was the one who had taken such care in setting up his new home. He definitely liked her very much, and looked forward to seeing her at meal times and whenever else he could squeeze in a moment with her. He wondered what she thought of him, and the sound of her singing filled his head as he fell asleep that night.

The next few days passed by with plenty of work on the barn. In fact, Sarah and the others only saw the menfolk at meals. She had to admit to herself that she missed talking with John. Her father retired earlier than normal that night directly after supper, and John was nice enough to help wash up. She offered him a hot cup of rose-hip tea by the fireside, as she readied Hope and Noah for bedtime. With the younger ones fast asleep, she joined John in the main room. She had been softly singing a good night song for the children, and he had listened with great joy from his chair by the fire,

"Sarah, I wanted to say thank you for making me so at home. I love being here, and sharing life with your family. Sure, your father may be a bit brusque, but he means well, and is very protective of you as a father should be. I couldn't help but overhear your singing the children to sleep. It was very beautiful. I would be honored to come to service to hear you sing if I may? Am I allowed as an outsider to attend?" he inquired.

"Yes, John, all are welcome. You will be seated on one side, along with all the other single men. You will fit in, because they do not yet have beards. Those are for the married men only," she giggled slightly as she imagined John taking part in the Amish service. It rotated from house to house every Sunday, "My father will like that you are wanting to attend our service. He will be impressed, and I already know that he values all your arduous work. He told me so just yesterday morning as he left for the general store," confided Sarah. John had been working double time to make certain that the barn would be ready on time. He also hoped Mr. Williams might need him to care for the animals, since he was responsible for tending the store. John would like to stay on, sharing in their lives, and he would be willing to learn how to tend to the animals and any farm work for her father. It was getting late, and John stood to make his way across the yard to his room. "Sarah," he asked nervously, "Would it be appropriate for you to walk with me to the shack?"

"Well, father is asleep, so I do not see any problem with that," she agreed tentatively. She had grown to really admire John, and hoped he would stay on and perhaps be happy here. But, she knew that he was an Englischer, and would always remain an outsider. She also knew that she could never entertain the idea of him courting her, as she was expected to court an Amish man. It was time for her to be looking for her own husband, as she was of age, and this was the Amish tradition. She put the thought out of her mind, and got up to walk John back to his tiny home.

As they walked together, John looked up at the starry sky, and commented on the cool night, "Are you warm enough, Sarah? If not, please take my coat," as he noticed her shiver in the moonlight. He loved the way she always blushed in his presence. He hoped that Sarah felt for him as much as he felt for her. For he was already falling in love with her, but knew he must tread very carefully, in order to keep Jacob a happy and trusting man.

"Would you sing a hymn for me, Sarah?" asked John, as he looked at her by the starlight, "It is allowed if it is a hymn, honoring Gott, as you say," and they grinned at his use of the Amish expression.

"I guess it would be ok," she said, and she chose the very same song that she had been singing that day he entered the general store. John listened to every lilt of her voice, and suppressed his urge to kiss her. That would have been too soon, and he was determined to make no gestures that she may not expect, though he sensed she might be hoping for the same thing. However, there was the issue of John not being part of the Amish faith, and this was going to present a huge problem if he were to act upon his feelings. He couldn't help but take her hand in his as they reached his door. Sarah stopped her song rather abruptly, and shied away from John immediately. He felt he had blundered the moment, but she did not run off,

"I am sorry to make you uncomfortable, Sarah. It's just that you sing so beautifully and sweetly, that it fills my heart with such happiness. I understand that I am not of your faith, but there is something I must speak to your father about before the end of the month. I am considering joining the Amish in life and in faith. I want to be worthy of your affections, as you must have guessed by now, my dear little songbird. I cannot bear not to hear your lovely singing. It is too bad that the Amish do not allow singing for secular purposes, but I can understand why."

Sarah stood somewhat aghast at John's admission of love, though she returned his feelings wholeheartedly. She would like nothing so much in this world as to be able to love John, but there were obvious hurdles that would have to be addressed, "John, it is very uncommon for an outsider to join the Amish ways, but it is not unheard of. We have never had one in our small community, but I have heard tale of it in larger ones," she stated confidently. Did she dare allow herself to love him back? This was a question that would have to wait. They said their good nights, and John watched as she got to her front door safely. John was more than a little intimidated at the thought of having to discuss becoming Amish with Jacob. He resolved to have that conversation before this Sunday. With that settled in his mind, John fell to sleep, and dreamed a beautiful dream of Sarah running through the meadow singing for all of nature and Gott to hear.

Over the next few days, John waited for an opportune time to broach the subject of his intentions to join the Amish. After working a bit later than usual, John and Jacob finally sat down upon the workbench, and John tried his best to engage Jacob in normal pleasantries. After a short while, John decided to tell Jacob what he wished to do,

"Mr. Williams, sir, I have treasured my time here working with you, and living side by side with your wonderful family. There is something very important that I wish to speak with you about."

"Yes, John, what is this that you need to discuss at this late hour?" replied Jacob.

"I understand that we are both very tired, and the hour is rather late, but this is something that is weighing heavily upon my mind, and something that I must speak with you about, and I prefer that we do so alone," offered John.

"Alright, then. Out with it. What is so important, John?"

"I have given this much thought, and I admire your way of life, and the way that your faith enters into every aspect of life. I have noticed how it makes me feel closer to Gott, and I want to join the faith. I realize that this is a rarity, but it is all that I want. You are an intelligent and observant man, Mr. Williams, and you must have noticed my affection for your lovely Sarah. I know that I cannot ask for her hand unless I am an Amish man. I seek to enter the Amish religion not just for the sake of Sarah, but for my own well-being. I want to fully belong to this community, and I want to worship and live just as you do," said John with as much earnestness as he could muster.

"Mr. Anders, though your intentions seem true and honest to me, you are correct in thinking that an Englischer cannot possibly enter into marriage with my daughter. I will speak to the men of the church before Sunday, but I must warn you that you are about to take on a long and serious obligation to Gott," answered Jacob, much to John's relief. This answer was what he was desperately hoping to hear from Sarah's father. It was proof, however small, that he accepted John as a suitor for Sarah once he converted to the Amish faith. It was something important he would be doing for himself and for Sarah. He had been practicing something special for Jacob, and now seemed the perfect time to say it. John stood up, and without further ado, launched into the Pennsylvania Dutch phrase he had been studying since he arrived. For it was on that very day, that John already knew that he must win the love of Sarah if he was ever to be a happy man,

"Mer sott em sei Eagne net verlosse; Gott verlosst die Seine night," and that is what John said right then and there to Jacob, which translated to "One should not abandon one's own; God does not abandon his own."

Jacob looked like the most surprised man on the face of the earth. Not only had John come to him in the hopes to become Amish, but he had made the effort to speak to him in the Old German. John couldn't have chosen a better phrase for the occasion, and Jacob could not deny John his dreams. Jacob resolved to speak to the other Amish, and begin John's training, "Yes, John. I am very pleased with your dedication to both Gott and my daughter. You shall be worthy of Sarah soon, so you may as well tell her of your intentions, before she sets eyes on another eligible bachelor," he chuckled. John had never seen Jacob smile before, let alone chuckle!

The next day, being Friday morning, John awoke at his normal time with his whole heart bursting with excitement. He wanted very badly to tell Sarah of the conversation that he and her father had had the night before, but he also wanted to choose just the perfect time to tell her. He had it thought out, and he hoped everything went according to plan. He would keep everything a secret from Sarah until tonight.

The day seemed endless to John, as he toiled away at his work. No matter how hot the day became, or how tired he felt, he felt an overwhelming sense of peace come over him, knowing he would eventually become a part of the community he had grown to love in such a short amount of time. Not only had he found a home and a new life filled with hope, he had also found the love of his life, who shared his love of music and singing. It filled him with absolute joy knowing that he was embarking on this new chapter in his life. As the sky darkened with the coming of dusk, John and Jacob stopped work. It was finally time for the family to have supper together. John's most favorite time of the day.

John explained to Jacob that he wanted to wash up and tidy himself before coming into the house for supper, so Jacob certainly sensed what was coming. He was happy for his daughter, but sad to lose her when she eventually married. Hope would have to take over the motherly duties of caring for her boppli bruder, but she had been well trained by her older sister.

Sarah served up the supper, and everyone took their place at the table. Everyone appeared to be hungry, and both her father and John remarked how delicious the chicken pot pie had turned out. She had handpicked the vegetables that she added to the chicken, and she did admit to herself that it tasted quite fresh and hearty. Right on schedule, Jacob excused himself saying that he was worn out. John helped with the cleaning up as he often did, and then Sarah helped put Hope and Noah to bed, but not without singing a soft and heartwarming bedtime song of "Lavender's Blue." John closed his eyes as he listened to her angel voice. His mother had once sung him the very same lullaby when he was just a small child. It made him feel happy, yet sad that his mother would not get the chance to meet his beloved, or hear her wonderful singing voice.

Sarah emerged from the back bedroom, and joined John by the fire as was their new custom. John said he was feeling very tired, and that it was high time he got to bed, for tomorrow was Saturday, and there was much work to be done on the barn. He asked Sarah to walk with him, and so she did. John and Sarah strolled through the garden pathway towards his shack that had been transformed into a humble home. John said he had heard her singing the delicate lullaby to her sister and brother, and asked her to sing it once again for him as they sat down on the garden bench. Sarah was not surprised at his request, as she knew that John adored her singing. After she had finished the song, John got down upon his knee. Sarah could barely comprehend what was happening, since she was totally unaware of John's important conversation with her daed. John looked into Sarah's big brown eyes, and said what he had been waiting to say to her all night long,

"My dearest Sarah, I have taken the liberty to speak to your father about joining the Amish, and he has agreed that I shall begin my lessons this Sunday service. So, that being settled, I am now worthy of the question I am about to put to you. After my lessons have concluded, and I have become fully Amish, please be my wife. I must have you as my very own, and I shall want to hear you sing to our own future children the special lullaby you have just finished singing to me this night. I love you with all of my heart."

Sarah looked at him, her eyes welling with emotion, as she grabbed hold of his shoulders to hug him snugly in her arms,

"Yes, John, there is nothing in the world that would be more wonderful than becoming your wife! I have felt this since you first surprised me in daed's store."

And so, the two young lovers walked happily to John's little house, dreaming of their future together in the not so distant future...

Ephesians 5:19 "...speaking to one another with psalms, hymns, and songs from the Spirit. Sing and make music from your heart to the Lord..."

Love In Amish Land

DEE SCOTT

Chapter One

Rows of black buggies and waiting horses were parked around the small white farm house. In the front yard, little boys ran through the grass, chasing one another across the damp April ground.

John Yoder watched the children from his kitchen window. Occasionally, a fellow-Amish man would walk behind him and give him a pat on the back. Their gentle words of comfort did nothing to ease the pain in John's heart.

"Sarah is in a better place now," one of the men told him before they said their goodbyes.

Yes, Sarah was in a better place now. John knew that. After six months of watching his wife wither away, her body slowly consumed by the fast-spreading cancer, he knew that she was finally at peace. Caring for her as she writhed in pain had done more to age John than he wanted to admit.

"Good things are coming," an Amish woman tried to assure him as she gathered her children to leave.

That morning they had finally put Sarah in the soft spring ground. Her body would rest in the Amish cemetery now – her spirit finally free from all she had endured.

One by one the other Amish gathered their families and left John's home. And as night closed in, he found himself all alone.

John made his way to the kitchen where he sat down at the table with a cold cup of coffee.

He and Sarah would have been married for twenty years that spring. He took a sip of his coffee. In all that time, John had held a secret in his heart. A secret he hoped that Sarah had never discovered.

A knock on the front door brought John to his feet.

"Who could that be?" he wondered aloud. At eight-thirty, he was certain it was too late for any of the other Amish to be calling.

When John opened the door, he couldn't help but take a deep breath. On the front porch stood a young man he could hardly recognize.

"*Daed*," the voice of the stranger sounded familiar, "I've come home, *Daed*."

Even though he was sporting a pair of blue jeans and a tee-shirt, it certainly was John's only son.

"Sam..."John didn't think he could find the right words to say. He opened the door wider and waited on his son to come inside.

"I heard about Mom," Sam muttered softly, "I am so sorry..."

John reached out an arm and put it on his son's shoulder, "Have you been doing okay, out there in the *Englisher* world?"

Sam took a deep breath, "I'm sorry I left, *Daed*. It wasn't fair to leave you here alone. I just couldn't stand to watch her suffer like that."

John knew that his son spoke the truth. Although Sam had always been a bit of a rebel, it was his mother's sickness that finally drove him away from the Amish community.

"I needed to get away."

John nodded slowly, "*Jah*, I understand."

"I'm not home for good." Sam whispered softly, "I'm only here to see you. I needed a fresh start, *Daed,* and I think I've found one. Maybe you could use a fresh start too?"

John opened his eyes in surprise. Leave the community? Leave the faith? Was his son serious?

"I couldn't...." John started, but then stopped short. He'd already fooled enough people. He'd been playing the part of a liar for twenty years. Maybe it was time for something new.

He took a deep breath and started again, "When do we leave?"

Chapter Two

Leaving behind everything had been difficult for John. He didn't tell anyone that he was going. He simply got in his son's shiny new car the next morning and left. Something about leaving behind his farmhouse felt good. John wouldn't miss it.

Sam lived in a nice apartment and had a job working at a factory making tires for cars.

John knew that he had to do some kind of work or he would drive himself crazy simply sitting in his son's empty apartment. Sam had a quick answer to his job dilemma.

"You could be a driver!" Sam suggested, "Just like we used to hire drivers when we were in the Amish community; many people in the city don't have their own vehicles and need someone to get them to work or appointments."

"I could never drive," John scoffed, "A buggy perhaps but not a car!"

Despite John's uncertainty, his son was persistent. Sam was determined that his father would learn how to drive and that he would get a job providing others with transportation.

When Sam wasn't working at the factory, he would help his dad learn how to drive.

While the city life helped to keep John distracted somewhat, nights were still long and difficult. He had a hard time sleeping; instead, he would stare at the ceiling, thinking about Sarah and wishing that he could have been a better husband to her.

Sarah had been so sweet, so kind, and so gentle to him.

But John had never loved her.

Not really.

In his heart, he reserved that love for a girl he had lost many years ago.

Emily.

Even thinking about her name still brought tears to his eyes. John had spent the last twenty-one years missing her. Every day, he had awoken and wished that she was the one by his side.

Poor Sarah had deserved better. But try as he might, Emily had always been on his mind and in his heart.

Sometimes he still found himself wishing that he could understand why she had left him. One day, they had been so close – and then she had faded out of his life. Their summer sunshine had quickly turned winter cold.

As John wiped tears from his eyes, he wished that he could start his entire life over. Maybe that's what the city would do for him. Maybe it truly could be a fresh start. Maybe he could put the ghosts of the past away once and for all.

Chapter Three

After living in the city for three months, John Yoder had seen his life change in so many ways. At Sam's persistence, he had done away with his Amish clothes and traded them in for a pair of jeans and a button-up shirt. His beard had been shaved away and his hair cut more like an *Englisher*.

But, no matter what John did to try to escape his past, it felt like he was constantly haunted by the ghosts of what could have been and what should have happened.

With a little practice, John soon got his driver's license and was able to get around the city with ease. Using a minivan, he advertised his services and made a lot of money taking people from place to place. It was so strange to be the one driving rather than the passenger!

"I wonder what is happening back home?" John thought to himself as he pulled up to a small apartment and waited on his passenger to come out.

He never knew who he was likely to pick up. Sometimes he drove teenagers to the mall, other times impoverished mothers and their children to doctor appointments, and other times he ended up taking drunken people home from parties.

John tapped his fingers on the steering wheel as he waited on his next client.

It had been three months to the day since Sarah had passed. Each day, John was constantly overwhelmed by the guilt of what he had done.

The sliding door opened before John even realized that his passenger had arrived.

"I need to go to the supermarket," a woman's voice spoke up softly with directions.

Something about her voice...John could hardly believe his ears. He was almost too afraid to even turn around and look, but forced himself to glance in the rear view mirror.

Sitting in the backseat of his blue minivan was a petite brown-haired woman who appeared to be in her mid-thirties. She was dressed in Amish clothing and was busy fumbling for something in her black bag.

Emily.

It had to be her. Even after all these years, she still looked the same.

John felt as if his heart would beat out of his chest. Grabbing for his sunglasses, he scrambled to put them on and cover more of his face than what was already hidden beneath his ball cap.

Could it really be her? John would almost swear that it was, but started to wonder if the stress of life was simply getting to him. Perhaps his troubled mind had begun to play tricks on him.

As he turned the van onto the highway, John announced, "I don't see many Amish people in this town."

His passenger gently laughed and said, "I suppose not. I'm probably the only one. Not many Amish live in towns."

"What brought you here?"

John knew that he had over-stepped his bounds. This woman, be it Emily or not, didn't know him from Adam. No Amish woman would want to tell all her personal stories to a man she hardly knew.

She was silent for a moment and then announced, "I haven't always lived in the city. But things change."

"I used to live near some Amish out in the country." John revealed, hoping to catch some sort of information that would tell him if this truly was his Emily from so long ago.

"Hmmm..." was all that she said.

The ride to the grocery store was very quiet, but John felt as if his heart was beating loud enough to hear it. He wanted so desperately to say something, to ask this woman her name, to discover if she truly was the woman he had loved with all his heart, but didn't know where to start.

As he waited for her to get out of the grocery store, John tapped his finger restlessly on the steering wheel, wondering what he should say.

"Well, I'm ready to go home," the Amish woman announced as she opened the van door and loaded up her few bags of groceries.

John started the engine and waited for her to settle back in the seat.

"No where else?" He asked, hoping that another stop would give him a chance to say something to her.

"No. Just home."

John glanced back in the rear view mirror, watching her as he pulled out of the parking lot. The ride home was just as quiet as the trip to the store.

When he pulled up to the apartment building, John swallowed hard, searching for something to say.

Before he could open his mouth, she asked, "Could you possible take me to the chiropractor in the morning?"

John didn't have to look at his schedule. He already knew the answer.

"Sure," he said, "What time?"

"Eight-thirty?" She asked.

John nodded his head and she gave a slight smile, "Then I'll see you tomorrow." She got out of the van and started to close the door before announcing, "Just so you'll know, my name is Emily."

Chapter Four

John couldn't believe that he had found her once again. He had been certain that Emily would be out of his life forever. He had only prayed for such a chance to come again.

But with the joy of his new discovery came the sickening reality that there was no hope for the future. Emily had left him before and, no matter how much time had passed, there was no reason that she wouldn't leave him again.

With Emily's memory came plenty of good thoughts but also terrible, deep pain. Just the realization of how much he had missed her brought on a new round of guilt. Poor Sarah. He had tried to be such a good husband to her but felt as if he had failed. He had never loved her the same way that he had loved Emily.

The next morning he picked Emily up for her appointment and wondered if he should tell her that he would be too busy to ever drive her again but, try as he might, he couldn't get the words to come out of his mouth.

"So," she settled back in the van seat after giving him directions to her chiropractor, "Tell me about yourself. I don't even know your name."

"It's..." John took a deep breath, "Jay."

"What is your life like, Mr. Jay?"

It was strange to think of Emily being so bold with a total stranger...especially someone she thought was an *Englisher*.

"I live with my son," he started awkwardly, "He has a little apartment on the edge of town. He works in a factory and I drive people."

John watched her nod in the rear view mirror.

"Do you have any children?" he ventured to ask.

Emily smiled sadly and shook her head, "No. I have no children. I have never been married."

Something about those words brought a lump to John's throat. He was happy to know that his true love had not given her affection to another and yet, knowing that she had left him for someone else would have been better than simply having her leave for no reason at all.

"Where is your wife?" She suddenly asked.

John took a deep breath, "She died...it's been three months. She had cancer for a long time. She battled it off and on all her life, but this time the cancer won the battle."

"I am so sorry," Emily whispered. Her voice sounded so genuine. So like John remembered from long ago. It felt like you could hear her heart pouring out in her words, "Sorry that you had to go through that. Losing someone dear to you can be hard. I know that for a fact."

John was surprised to realize that they had already reached the chiropractor's office. The ride had been so pleasant; he could hardly believe how fast the time had passed.

The wait seemed like it took hours, but Emily came out with a smile on her face.

"Anywhere else?" John asked.

When Emily shook her head no, John took a bold move, "Would you mind if I stop for a cup of coffee and a donut?"

"Of course not!" She assured him.

John pulled into a small donut shop and hurried inside. He went up to the counter and ordered two strawberry donuts and two cups of coffee.

"Oh," Emily exclaimed as he handed her one of the coffees and a donut, "You shouldn't have done that!"

"It's my treat."

"You made a good choice," she announced as she took a bite of the gooey treat, "Strawberry is my favorite. I used to make them all the time."

John could remember the picnics that they had together by the river. Emily had always brought a batch of her homemade donuts. Somehow the one he was eating tasted bland in comparison to the wonderful-good memory.

When John took Emily to her apartment, she pulled out her checkbook and asked, "How much for the ride?"

"No charge." He announced.

"You can't work for nothing," she started to protest but he stopped her.

"I got a donut and some coffee. That was plenty."

Emily smiled and cocked her head to the side, "Thanks then. I'll get back with you."

John watched as she stepped out of the van and started toward her apartment. She had said nothing else about another ride. Was this to be the last time he would see her?

"Please, God," he prayed softly, "Let me see this dear woman again!"

Her smile hadn't changed. It had been twenty-one years since he last saw it and it felt like a step back in time. A little lopsided, but beautiful.

As he drove back to his son's apartment, John remembered the day that he first saw that smile. He had been eighteen years old. John had been dating Sarah for two years and he was thinking about asking her to be his wife. That summer Sarah had left to go stay with her aunt in Indiana, leaving John completely alone. One of the Amish families was hosting a gathering for the young people and Emily had been there visiting from a nearby community.

Emily was sixteen-years-old with curly dark hair and a sparkle in her eyes. When she first looked at John and smiled, he was instantly smitten. Suddenly, all thoughts of Sarah were gone as he fell madly in love with this younger girl.

He had sent Sarah a letter, explaining that it was time for them to take a break from their relationship and had then pursued Emily. They had great times together. He could remember sitting outside of the young peoples' meetings on his buggy, so full of things to say to each other that they couldn't force themselves to go inside and enjoy the fun. They had counted stars together, made wishes together, and dreamed of the future.

Then summer had come to an end. And, as quickly as she had appeared, Emily was gone. John had sent her one letter after another but she never replied. He had even gone to her house but she wouldn't come to the door.

When Emily was gone, Sarah reappeared. Sarah was familiar and stable. She was there to distract him from Emily. And, once John realized that Emily would never come back, he was ready to take the step forward and not only renewed their relationship but asked Sarah to marry him.

Even though Sarah became John's wife, he never loved her. Not like he had loved Emily.

Chapter Five

The next four days were difficult. All John could do was think about Emily. It felt that he had lost her once again. The pain was almost too much to bear. His mind was filled with her memories and, with those memories came a flood of guilt and confusion.

John would never understand why Emily had left him all those years ago. Had he done something wrong? Had she never truly loved him at all? Had he simply been used by a girl who wanted a beau for the summer?

And, worse yet, came the reality that he even cared. After all that had happened, he should have forgotten all about his old sweetheart. After twenty years of marriage, he should be mourning the loss of his wife.

John was sitting at the kitchen table, reading the newspaper when his phone began to ring.

"Hello," he answered the call from an unknown number.

"Hello Mr. Jay. It's Emily."

He didn't even have to hear her name to know who it was. John's heart skipped a beat and he found himself standing up in surprise, "Yes?"

"How are you?" She asked somewhat awkwardly.

"Oh, I'm doing well. Just waiting on my son to get home from work. Do you need to go somewhere?"

"No, I don't need a ride."

When he realized that he would not be able to see her, John felt a lump rise in his throat.

Before he could say anything else, Emily jumped ahead, "If you're not busy, would you like to come by for supper? It would make me feel good to repay you for the ride you gave me the other day."

John could hardly believe his ears. Emily was inviting him over for supper?

"What time?" He asked quickly.

"The food will be ready at five, but you can come earlier if you want."

"I'll be there!" John exclaimed. Hanging up the phone, John glanced at his watch and started preparing for the evening ahead.

He arrived at Emily's apartment at four-thirty.

Initially, things seemed cold and formal but, before long, they were laughing together. As strange as the situation seemed, it felt like John had gone back in time. Although Emily had aged over the last twenty-one years, she was still the same carefree girl who had stolen John's heart.

John helped her to prepare the meal and they laughed together when she left the rolls in the oven for too long and burnt them.

"Delicious," John announced as he took a bit of the pork roast and washed it down with some homemade lemonade.

"I learned from my mom," Emily announced with a smile.

"Is your family okay with you living here...alone...away from the community?" John asked suddenly, surprised that Emily was staying in an apartment by herself with electricity and other things from the *Englisher* world.

Emily shook her head sadly, "No. They are not happy at all. But they have grown used to it." She reached out and began clearing away some of the empty dishes, "I've been here alone for the past fifteen years."

John wanted to ask so many questions but all he could get out was, "Why?"

"You know, Mr. Jay," Emily took a deep breath and then started her story, "I am not married, but it's not because I don't want to be."

"You have a boyfriend?" John quickly asked.

Emily smiled tiredly and said, "No. Nothing like that. I had a beau once. I thought we would get married, really. I met him at a young peoples' meeting for the Amish and we spent the whole night talking. I felt as if I had met my soul-mate and, the more time we were together, the more certain I became."

Her voice trailed off and John found himself struggling to maintain his composure.

"Mr. Jay," she sighed sadly, "I loved that boy. I loved my John so deeply. I would not have given him up for anyone else." She shook her head and looked down at her hands.

"What happened?" John choked out the words.

"He already had a girlfriend," Emily whispered, "Her name was Sarah and she was one of my distant cousins. When he broke up with her to court me, I didn't realize how deeply it would hurt her. She was in a different state for the summer. In my mind, I thought she surely didn't love John as much as I. At least, I felt that way until she came to visit me. She look horrible, Mr. Jay. Her eyes were swollen and her face hollow. She was always a sickly girl. She told me that John had loved her and that her heart was broken."

At this point, tears were flowing down Emily's face as she finished her story, "I couldn't do it to her. I couldn't take away this girl's entire world. So, I left. I went back home and I never spoke to John again. For a while, he sent me letters. I burnt them. It hurt me too much to think of reading his dear writings. He came to see me but I wouldn't accept him. I stayed away from him. I knew that, if I was to see his face again, it would break my heart. I loved him so much. That's why I left my Amish community. My family wanted me to marry someone else, but I couldn't. That's why I'm here at this apartment. I would rather live alone than live with someone else."

"All these years," Emily's voice was now no more than a whisper, "I have wanted to tell John the truth. I want him to know how much he means to me. I have wanted to let him know why I left."

John opened his mouth to say something. He wanted to reach out and pull Emily to him, but was stopped short by the ringing of his cell phone. John almost ignored it until he saw that it was his son.

"Sam?" He asked, surprised to see that his son had called him.

"Dad," the voice on the other end of the line was shaky, "I'm at the emergency room."

Suddenly, all his thoughts were on his son. John left Emily alone with a sad smile and a quick explanation, and then hurried away to the hospital to see what had happened to his son.

Chapter Six

"I didn't mean for you to rush over to get me," Sam laughed as John stood over his son's bed in the emergency room, "I just need someone to take me home. I don't even think I need to be here...I would have kept working but the boss insisted I get checked out."

"What happened?"

Sam smiled and shook his head before wincing, "Oh, I just tripped and hit my head really good on a piece of machinery."

John breathed a sigh of relief and sat down in the chair next to the hospital bed. This day had been almost too much for John to handle.

He covered his face with his hands. He had been so afraid that he was going to lose his son. Now, he was overwhelmed with emotion. He was so thankful that Sam was going to be okay, but found himself forced to focus on his visit with Emily.

He now knew the truth. Emily hadn't stopped loving him. She had given him up out of love for him. She had cared for Sarah and wanted to make sure she had a happy life.

What now?

John was almost thankful that Sam had called him away from the uncertain situation. He wasn't sure what he would have done or said if his phone hadn't interrupted his visit with Emily.

"Where were you anyway?" Sam asked as he reached up to gingerly pat his injured head, "I would have sworn I heard a woman talking in the background. Were you watching television?"

Sam should have known that his dad had little use for the television that was in his apartment. John shook his head 'no" and muttered, "It was just a friend."

"A friend?" Sam repeated in surprise, "Dad, I didn't know that you had friends...let alone lady friends. Obviously I need to spend a little less time at work and a little more keeping up with my *daed*!"

John rolled his eyes and tried to act unconcerned; however, he felt completely awkward and ill-at-ease.

"So, who was she?" Sam teased with a smile.

"No one." John answered sharply, "No one at all. Just an old friend."

Sam lifted his eyebrows and then winced when the movement made his head hurt.

"Dad...what's this about? Are you seriously seeing a woman?"

"Don't talk that way," John started, "Your mom just in the grave..."

"Dad," Sam's voice was serious now and he looked John straight in the eyes, "You took *gut* care of mom. You always provided for her and me, and you gave us a good life. But I could tell things were never right..."

John lowered his eyes in shame. All these years he had tried so hard to put on a good show and make everyone think he had felt more for Sarah than he truly had.

"Don't be ashamed," Sam assured him, "I can understand. You were faithful and good to us for all those years. But Mom's gone now. Your time with her is over…maybe it's time for you to really be with someone who makes you happy."

The voice of the doctor interrupted them as he pulled back the curtain and stepped into the room. Once again, John was saved an awkward conversation but he felt somehow disappointed. He felt as if he needed to talk to someone and his son's words made him feel better about all his choices throughout the years.

Just as Sam had predicted, there was nothing wrong with him. He had a goose egg on his head, but no serious damage. The doctor released him from the hospital and John drove him home in his van.

Once they were back at Sam's apartment, he sat down to watch some television while John fixed a frozen pizza that he found in the freezer.

"Thanks," Sam announced as he reached for the pizza his dad offered him.

"Sam," John sat down across from him and took a deep breath. He was so overcome by uncertainties that he needed to talk to someone.

Sam turned off the TV and gave his dad his full attention.

"Sam," John started again, "When I came to town with you, I was hoping to get away from all my mistakes. I have made many mistakes. Just like you said, I never had deep feelings for your mother. I spent my entire life pining away after a girl who left me when I was eighteen years old. Her name was Emily and I loved her all these years. Imagine how surprised I was when I found her right in this very town. Sam, I've been trying to get over her memory and forgive myself for not treating your mother better, but now I'm not sure what to do."

Sam's eyes were huge. In a moment, all his questions had been answered and he finally understood his father.

"Does she still love you?" He asked in surprise.

"She still loves John Yoder. She doesn't know that I'm him. She thinks I'm a man simply named 'Jay'. I wanted to tell her the truth, but I couldn't."

Sam started blankly as if he couldn't believe his own ears, "Dad, you have to tell her the truth. She deserves to know. You've both been mooning around over each other all these years...you and she both deserve some kind of closure."

John shook his head slowly, "I wouldn't even know where to start..."

"*Daed*," Sam reached out and patted his father's arm, "Just tell her the truth. Tell her what's in your heart."

Chapter Seven

John had never been as nervous in his life. He stood on the apartment porch, shifting from one foot to the other as he tried to gather enough courage to knock on the door. Slowly, he lifted a knotted fist and gave a sturdy rap against the wooden frame.

What would Emily say when she found out the truth? Would she be angry at him for hiding who he truly was? Would she be disenchanted to see the man that he had become?

Obviously she wasn't coming to the door. Perhaps she had left. Evening was starting to close in; maybe she had gone to bed.

John let out a sigh of mixed relief and disappointment, and started to turn. Suddenly, the door swung open and Emily was standing in front of him. She looked at him in surprise, her head cocked slightly to the side.

"You're back." She announced.

"Yes, I'm back."

"I was afraid that you were gone for good. How is your son?"

"He's fine." John took a deep breath, "Can I come inside?"

Emily stepped back and motioned for him to come into her apartment. She led him to a recliner and sat down on the couch next to him.

"I have something I need to tell you," John began awkwardly.

Emily looked at him expectantly, but he couldn't force the words to come.

"Yes?" She tried to nudge him along.

"Tonight, you told me a story about your old boyfriend..." John started only to stop himself and begin again, "I haven't always lived here. I've not always been a driver..."

He stopped and looked at Emily. She sat so close to the edge of the couch, he could reach out and touch her if he was bold enough. She stared at him, her dark eyes wide and questioning.

John couldn't handle it any longer, "I don't know how to begin to tell you this, but Emily...I am John Yoder."

The silence in the room was almost deafening. Emily opened her mouth and then shut it. John tried to read her expression, but he couldn't see past the tears that were forming in his eyes.

She took a deep breath, her chest rising and falling, as she gathered her composure.

"I shouldn't have come," John announced as he grabbed the chair arm and started to push himself up, "I am so sorry. I shouldn't have said a thing."

In an instant, Emily reached out a hand and put it on his, urging him to stay seated.

John relaxed back in his seat, surprised at her gesture.

She leaned forward in her seat and reached out to cup his face in her hand, "Oh, John," she whispered. The tenderness in her voice revealed twenty years of pain that had been waiting for a release, "Don't you realize that I've known it all along?"

John could feel his eyebrows rise in shock. Emily had known who he was the entire time? How was it possible?

Emily pulled her hands back and began to clasp them together on her lap, "Someone told me about a driver named John Yoder. I wasn't sure that it was you, but I had to call and see. John, I have waited so long to see you again. After what I told you today, I was so afraid that you wouldn't come back. I was afraid that you didn't care for me anymore. I was afraid that you would be angry or disgusted or..." Her soft voice trailed off and her words were replaced by her soft sobs.

Before he knew what he was doing, John was by her side on the couch. He reached out and enveloped her in his strong arms, pulling her close to him. He couldn't believe that this moment was real.

The past twenty years felt as if they had never happened as Emily returned his embrace. He leaned his chin against her shoulder, soaking in the smell of her lavender soap.

"Emily," He whispered her name over and over, "Dear, sweet Emily. I think I love you more now than ever."

"Then you don't hate me?" She sobbed, "After I left you, I thought you would hate me."

"I could never hate you!" John exclaimed, "You were nothing but a girl trying to do what was best for those you loved. I am only angry at myself for not caring more for Sarah. She was a good wife and you sacrificed yourself to make sure that she was happy."

Emily reached up to wiped her eyes, "Wait just a minute. I have to get something to show you."

John didn't want to let her go. He wanted to hold her in his arms forever, but he released her long enough for her to run into a back room and hurry back, a piece of paper in her hand.

"John, you need to read this."

With trembling hands, John took the piece of paper and began to read to himself.

"Dearest Emily,

I don't know how to start this letter to you. It has been twenty years since we last spoke. I still remember begging you to break things off with John so that he would marry me...it seems a lifetime ago.

I have had a good life Emily. The Lord blessed us with a beautiful son named Sam. He is now nineteen years old and has left the Amish faith. I continue to pray that he will leave the *Englisher* world and return home in good time.

As you know, I have always been sick. I am now in the end stages of cancer. There is no cure and I am slowly fading away.

John has been a blessing to me. No one could ever ask for a dearer, sweeter man. He spends every day by my side, and never lets me want for anything. No matter how tired he maybe, he is always ready to do what I need. I could not have ordered a better man.

I know that John still loves you. Every day, I can see the emptiness in his eyes. His heart has never been complete since you left him. And somehow, that makes his care for me even more precious. Even though I am not his soul-mate, he cares for me with his whole heart – which is an entirely different sort of priceless love. He may not love me as passionately as you, but I believe that he loves me as much simply in another way.

After twenty years of marriage, I find that it is now my turn to leave John. And, after years of my own selfish happiness, I want to give him back to you. Please, find him. Please, marry him. Make yourselves a happy life together.

With all my love,

Sarah"

John read the letter over and over again. Somehow, as he let those words sink into his heart, all of his guilt, pain, and resentment melted away.

It was true, he had loved Sarah; maybe not in the same romantic, passionate way that he loved Emily, but he had loved his wife. He knew that he could now forgive himself and move forward with his life.

"I have prayed so hard to find you, John." Emily whispered as she leaned her head against his shoulder.

John put his arm around her, pulling her tightly against his body.

"Emily," he choked out softly, "Will you be my wife? After all these years, will you still have me?"

Emily nodded her head, "Of course, John. That is what I want with my whole heart."

John lifted her chin with his thumb and tilted his head to the side. Leaning forward, his lips met hers. This was to be the first of many, many kisses to come.

Epilogue

John Yoder watched the children playing from his kitchen window. Rows of black buggies were parked in front of his house as groups of Amish families made their way toward the door. They were preparing for a work frolic to help John raise a new barn.

"What are you doing?" A soft voice whispered near his ear as Emily stepped up and put her arm around his waist.

"Just thinking, my love," he turned and pulled her closer to him.

So much had happened since that day a year ago when he had visited Emily in her apartment. Together they had returned to the Amish and were married together beneath the old oak tree in the front yard.

"There comes Sam," John announced with a smile as his son's black car pulled up into the driveway. Although Sam had yet to rejoin the Amish church, he came to frequently visit and help his father. John held out hope that Sam would eventually return to the faith and they could live their lives side-by-side.

"You'd better get out there and start to work," Emily stepped back, "I need to go check on baby Johnny."

John watched as his wife went to check on their newborn baby.

He had hoped for a fresh start after Sarah's death. His wish had been granted.

John smiled softly to himself. Life truly was good.

END

AMISH DAWN

AMANDA REESE

Chapter 1: Times Like This

Dawn Wittmer always thought of herself as a simple girl, and was a simple girl in the eyes of everyone, except her parents. Everything that Dawn did was wrong. How could it be that such a simple girl was never good at doing anything? Dawn knew that her parents were quite strict, but still, she wondered why she never earned their satisfaction. Her parents' disapproval came out in ways that she preferred not to consider, such as her poor self-esteem. Even when she was selling the family's produce in the market she found herself stressed and worried that she would do something wrong, give incorrect change, or lose customers by not providing the service and prices that the customers wanted.

Dawn knew so little about life; sometimes she wanted her world to be just at least a little bit bigger than the world that her parents imagined for her. Dawn would have loved to have permission to just be a little bit, well, "normal." Some of her other Amish friends had permission to go out of the house, have English friends, and even on a rare occasion have a beer or a glass of wine. She didn't want to leave the Amish community but recently the way her parents had been treating her like she was a 7-year-old again was making her go crazy and feel more anxious.

Dawn wasn't seven years old and she knew that very well. She was 18 years old and graduating school this year. She'd learned more from studying on her own than she gained from attending school in the one room schoolhouse that her parents insisted she attend. Dawn dreamed of attending university, of becoming a nurse, and helping those who were sick. She didn't agree with everything that the Amish believed, such as their views regarding medicine and the use of it. Why shouldn't those who are very sick utilize medicine if they have the chance to make use of modern medicine that could save their lives? Why did her parents have to see everything in "black and white?" Everything was always good or bad. In other words, everything was Amish or English and if it was English that meant it was not acceptable.

If her parents knew about her views on medicine or that sometimes she drank wine with her friends they would be so angry that she probably could not stay in their home. What was so terrible about having a glass of wine? She wanted to know. The smell of a nice glass of Merlot or Cabernet Sauvignon would make her evening. Just that little feeling that lifted her mood ever so slightly. She could feel the stress melt away from her heart, her head, her soul, her body with just one glass of wine. Sometime when she visited her friend Beth Troyer they would sit and play Scrabble together, passing the time, laughing, and talking. What neither her parents nor Beth's parents knew was that an English friend of Beth's would buy her wine. Sometimes she paid her friend with money if she had any, and other times with baked goods.

Beth understood Dawn. They had been friends since they were little and even though neither one wanted to consider leaving the Amish community they had some complaints with the rules. Why were there so many rules?

Chapter 2: Market Days

Dawn's life continued. Her days at the market were long. Secret Scrabble and wine nights were few and far between. Plus, it was hard for Beth to sneak the wine into her room and get it cold. There was almost no way to get the wine cold unless her English friend brought the wine already chilled and they consume it immediately.

Among the rows of sellers in the market were both English and Amish vendors. The cost of renting the space was increasing yet their sales remained more or less the same. The same customers. The weeks melted into each other, seeming almost entirely the same. She hardly had any schoolwork to do and she knew that her parents would never let her attend college. What was the point? Recently one of the other storefront owners was coming around to her store almost every day. It was almost annoying. Actually, it was annoying. Sunny Landsdale was his name. He was a fairly tall young man with wide shoulders, and his hair was pulled back in a ponytail, as if he wanted to be a girl. His name sounded much like a name for a girl too. She thought he was a little strange, but perhaps some part of him could be likeable. Dawn's thoughts drifted to her Amish upbringing. God asks us to love everyone, not just the people we like or love. Certainly, it was her job to treat everyone with respect that came to her stand, whether or not she liked her family's customers. She convinced herself to make small talk with Sunny. She even wanted to get up the nerve to ask him why he didn't cut his hair. Maybe today would be the day she would ask him.

Among the other fruit and pastry sellers, Dawn sat at her stand amid crates of tomatoes, cucumbers, onions, garlic, corn, and even carrots when Sunny approached the stand again. Perhaps more annoying than his hair was the fact that he stopped by more or less just to chat. He didn't seem to have any objective except bothering her! Was this the goal? This could hardly be the goal. Of course, it also seemed strange that he would come and buy just a single tomato or onion. He claimed that he bought fresh ingredients every day to cook dinner. Dawn presumed that although this could be true, he also apparently came around to her stand just to speak to her. Although many other people would consider this a compliment she preferred to do her work and be left alone. Not to mention that she had heard some interesting things about him. Some stories that she hoped were not true. She heard he had multiple lovers, all customers. She didn't want to hear anymore.

"My dearest Dawn, you are looking beautiful as always. Although I bet you would look stunning in a long, sleek, black evening gown! You are quite a beauty. What can I say?" said Sunny. "Well, you could say less. That would be a great start," replied Dawn. "Oh, my lovely, one day you will be my wife, just you see! But, in the meantime I will have to wait for you to choose to leave your Amish community and run away with me. Of course, a man cannot wait forever!" declared Sunny with enthusiasm. Dawn rolled her eyes and asked him, "So, what can

I get for you today, Mr. Landsdale: a single tom..." Sunny interrupted her midsentence. "I thought we discussed that my name is Sunny. Still you prefer to refer to me as Mr. Landsdale. Mr. Landsdale is my father, thank you very much."

"As you wish, Sunny," Dawn heard herself say. She couldn't help but thinking about how silly his name and hair were. Sunny laughed and Dawn paused before posing her question. "Mr. Landsdale, ahem, I mean, Sunny, did you ever realize that, between your hair and your name, some people may think some strange things about you. I don't mean to be rude, but you can hear all kinds of gossip about a boy with a name like Sunny!" Dawn offered this observation with some courage. Sunny simply laughed, "Actually, I love my name, and yes, my hair too. You wanted to ask about my hair, I'm sure. No?" asked Sunny. "Well, yes, I hadn't quite gotten there yet," said Dawn.

"Well, to tell you the truth, since you know, I'm always honest about everything, like your good looks for example... anyway, as I was saying. My Dad always cut my hair very short when I was a kid and I hated it. When I finally got old enough to make my own decisions about my hair, I decided to stop cutting it. My whole family went crazy, but then they got used to it, and I realized I actually quite liked it. So, I kept it. Now the hair goes better with my name too! It keeps people on their toes," answered Sunny.

"You certainly are at least an interesting person," answered Dawn. Sunny smiled as a slightly extended pause in the conversation ensued. "Right, anyway, I need three green peppers for dinner tonight," said Sunny. "Sure, wow. Three, not one?" joked Dawn. "Yes, three," echoed Sunny as a goofy grin spread across his face. Sunny handed over $1.00, took his green peppers and walked away back toward his stand.

Dawn found herself watching him as he walked away and couldn't understand what or why she was watching. He was such a strange man. Dawn shook her head and continued scouring the market, hoping to make eye contact with potential customers. Business had been slower than usual this summer with no thanks to the opening of a super Wal-Mart on the south side of the city. That's what she guessed anyway. It's difficult to maintain customers and gain new ones when giant corporations can roll into town and capitalize on the local people's inability to lower prices to an unreasonable point. As Dawn grew lost in her thoughts about the super Wal-Mart and even surprisingly about herself the market day grew to a close. She carefully put away all the unsold food, locked the cabinets, and made her way home by foot.

Chapter 3: A Patient Man

Jane and Mason Wittmer, Dawn's parents, did not see positive changes in Dawn. In fact, they were ready to sit down with their daughter and discuss with her their knowledge of this Sunny boy. Jane and Mason were respected by the entire Amish community and were well-known and respected even in the marketplace. It had come to their attention that Sunny Landsdale, a known associate of the Amish Mafia was purchasing goods from their store, which in and of itself, is not a crime. They did not appreciate, however, that he was making conversation with their daughter. Parents know best, of course. Anyone even vaguely connected with Amish Mafia was not a friend of theirs. They didn't like what they know about Sunny. They even considered removing Dawn from the market stand to keep Sunny away from her.

Jane and Mason decided that they needed to sit down with their daughter and discuss this situation that was ever so pressing on their minds. A good Amish daughter did her work, stayed away from unnecessary conversation with any English man, worked on the farm or in the market, prayed, and did her homework. Dawn could be quickly headed down the wrong path. On the evening following the day of the three green peppers, Jane and Mason decided to summon their daughter to the sitting area.

"Dawn!" Jane called up the stairs. "We need you to come downstairs for a minute." Dawn immediately knew that those words meant "we want to have a serious conversation with you." A million and one things were passing through Dawn's mind. Did they found out that she and Beth had been sneaking wine into the community and drinking sometimes? Will they forbid her to apply to college?

"Dawn. We want you to stay away from the Sunny boy," said Jane. "Any questions?" asked Mason, Dawn's father. Dawn stayed silent. "No comment at all?" inquired her mother. "Well, yes: you know it's not my fault who comes to buy food at our store. What, you want me to put out a sign that says only GOOD people buy food here! Are you crazy?" said Dawn. "Enough!" shouted Mason. "We just want you to be a little careful with Sunny. Don't make conversation. Give him what he purchases and be sure to count the change extra carefully. Okay?" said Jane.

"Sure, Mom... whatever," answered Dawn as she rolled her eyes without realizing what she was doing until it was too late. "Not whatever, do not talk to your Mom with that tone of voice, and don't let me see you roll your eyes again!" shouted Mason. "Yes, Dad. May I be excused?" "Yes, thank you Dawn," whispered Jane in a small voice.

As Dawn crept back up the winding wooden staircase to her room she considered the conversation. Although she was annoyed by the way they had accused her of engaging in conversation with Sunny, she was more relieved that they didn't know about the wine. She wasn't a drunk. She didn't need a drink. She just liked a glass of wine once in a while. That hardly made her a sinner, or evil, did it? She didn't think that made her a sinner. In the Bible, Mary asked Jesus to turn water into wine during a wedding when the couple ran out of wine to serve their guests. Dawn silently recounted the parable to herself and reminded herself that she was not a bad person. She simply had difficult, traditional Amish parents.

She continued working at the market after the confrontation with her parents. But as if he'd been warned away, Sunny was suddenly making himself scarce. She wondered where he had gone. Was he okay? She chided herself for thinking about whether or not he was okay. Why was she worried about Sunny? Sunny, his girlish name, his bleached pony tail, and cocky smile. What a silly man; no... what a silly boy. How old was he anyway? After a week of managing the store in the market and seeing no sign of Sunny, Dawn was just about ready to accept that he had found another girl to flirt with. Or, perhaps, he'd left town. Types like Sunny didn't usually stick around too long. But just then there was a tap on her shoulder. "Good afternoon, Ms. Wittmer. How are you today?" asked Sunny. "Just fine, thank you, but um... where have you been?" asked Dawn.

"Ah! So, you missed me, right? I knew it! I knew you'd miss me!" replied Sunny, a huge grin spreading across his face. "No, I didn't say that. I just said, where have you been?" retorted Dawn. "Of course, as you see it. Busy. That's all," replied Sunny. "Okay, so what can I get you today?" asked Dawn.

"Well, actually, I don't need any green peppers, but I did want to know if you'd like to accompany me for a smoothie!" invited Sunny in a bright, ironically sunny way. "You mean, um, like a date?" asked Dawn. "Yes. Or no. Whatever you would like it to be," replied Sunny. "You know, I'm not... um, I'll think about it," said Dawn. "You'll think about it. Okay: well, I can be a patient man. Let me know, let's say tomorrow, about our non-date. It's just a smoothie," Sunny pointed out diplomatically.

With that, Sunny turned and walked backed into the crowd of the market. Dawn found herself standing at the counter trying to catch her breath. Yes, for certain, Sunny had just asked her out on a date. Were her parents correct in saying to stay away from him? What if they were just wrong about him? It wouldn't be the first thing they were wrong about. She never had English friends before because her family forbid it. She was just curious enough what it would be like to go out with an English boy that she contemplated saying yes. As she closed the store for the day she found herself poised between her family's values and wanting to discover herself and the world for herself.

Chapter 4: More Than Just Coffee

The next day as Sunny approached the counter, without even thinking Dawn said, "Yes." Surprised, Sunny said, "Ok then, I'll be back at close to 4pm to meet you!" As Sunny turned to walk away, Dawn said, "Wait, make it 3pm outside the back entrance of the market." "Anything for my sunshine!" replied Sunny and laughed, since, after all, his name was sunshine, not hers. At precisely 3pm Dawn closed the store one hour earlier than usual and met him outside the market. Dawn found Sunny waiting for her there. "It's just a few blocks away," said Sunny.

As they walked Dawn realized she didn't know what to say at all. It was as if someone had glued her lips together. Sunny, recognizing the pause and potential awkwardness, started talking about himself. "Well, since you don't know a lot about me, I'll tell you the saga, if you want." "Sure," answered Dawn.

"I grew up in several different foster homes, bounced from one to another, and usually I ran away because my foster parents would beat or just use me for the government check. You know?" Sunny began his remarkable tale as if it were commonplace. "Actually, I'm sorry, I'm not understanding, because you know I'm Amish," admitted Dawn. Sunny started again, in an attempt to clarify: "When I was young, my parents died in a car accident. I was 4 years old. Just old enough to remember them and miss them. When you become an orphan, or your parents don't want you, the state tries to find a placement for you with another family in another home. But sometimes, these homes are dangerous. There aren't enough controls and regulations on who can become a foster parent." "Oh, I'm sorry. I had no idea," said Dawn. "Don't be. I'm just sharing with you my story. As soon as I turned 18 I was out of the system because I became a legal adult. I was homeless for a little while until I found a job at one of the stands here. They pay me cash under the table. No taxes or anything. Since then I've saved enough money to get a place, but I've never finished school. I want to get my GED someday, but that seems like a dream." said Sunny.

There was another pause in the conversation, but this time, perhaps it was a needed pause. "And now, how are you?" Dawn asked with genuine concern. "I'm well, just me," said Sunny. "But, why did you tell me this other story about your hair and your parents, when you don't have parents?" asked Dawn. "I wanted to impress you," Sunny confessed. "I didn't want you think I was just some orphan kid. In the beginning, I kept my hair long because my foster parents would rarely give me a haircut, let alone pay for me to get one. Sometimes they would destroy my hair when they cut it. So, finally, when I aged out of foster care, I decided nobody was going to cut my hair like that again, even me," explained Sunny.

"Well, anyway, that's me. How about those smoothies?" Sunny invited, apparently ready to change the subject. "Of course," said Dawn. As they sat together in the Tropical Smoothie Café, Dawn imagined that in some ways she had never considered before, she'd been given more opportunities in her strictly controlled life than an English man like Sunny. She wanted to tell him that her parents would freak out if they knew she had come out with him even for a smoothie, but then again, she thought it might be better if she said nothing. He probably could have guessed as much anyway. As they continued talking, Sunny moved his hand across the table and placed it on top of Dawn's hand. Dawn was startled and considered moving it. But she found that she didn't want to move it. Nobody in the Amish community would be this open with another. No one would tell someone else who wasn't in his or her family personal things. Why couldn't she trust Sunny? It was true he was two years older than she was, but two years was nothing. Plus, they were both legal adults, and hand-holding wasn't a crime.

Finally, Dawn got up the nerve to ask Sunny about the gossip at the market. "Sunny, can I ask you something?" Dawn inquired. "Sure," replied Sunny. "Is it true that you... you know... with other girls. Like am I just one of a bunch of other girls?" asked Dawn. "Oh, no... actually I just ignore the gossip at the market. One of my old foster parents owns a stall in the market so they made up stories about me to try to make me lose my job, but it didn't work," replied Sunny. "Oh, I thought... sorry," whispered Dawn. "Don't be, it's not a problem."

Just then Dawn looked at the clock on the wall and realized it was 4:20. If she didn't all but run home her parents would know something was up. Dawn jumped up and said a little louder than necessary, "Oh, I have to leave quickly... if I don't get home soon..." "It's a problem, right? Your parents I'm sure wouldn't like seeing someone like me with their daughter. Right?" interrupted Sunny. "Actually, yes I'm really sorry. Please. I have to go. I'll see you tomorrow at the market?" asked Dawn, "Yes, don't worry, just g,." replied Sunny.

Chapter 5: Learning to Fly

They knew. Before Dawn even made it inside the door, Jane and Mason were waiting for Dawn at the kitchen table. How could I be so stupid, thought Dawn. Of course, someone would have noticed that she closed the store an hour earlier. As Dawn approached her parents, her father started screaming, so loud, that even the neighbors on the opposite end of the community would hear him. She was positive. "Dawn. You're going to your uncle's! We're sending your disobedient soul away! You need to learn respect, and the importance of NOT LYING TO YOUR FAMILY! End of discussion! You will not go back to the marketplace tomorrow. You will not see Sunny Landsdale ever again! Do you hear me?" raged Dawn's father Mason.

Dawn stood in silence in the kitchen and held back tears. Mason continued screaming. "Do you know what filth people like Sunny are? He is nothing. Nobody. He is a cheater and he hangs around with the type of people we do NOT associate with! Do you understand me? We know for a fact that he has purchased a gun from the Amish Mafia. We don't know why he has a gun or wanted a gun, but you cannot speak to him ever again. ARE WE CLEAR?" bellowed Mason

Dawn could do nothing except nod her head yes. Then she ran to her room. She wanted to find Beth and tell her everything. She wanted even more to speak to Sunny. Her parents didn't understand him. They didn't know him. And if he owns a gun, Dawn was sure that there was a reason. Sunny was a good man. They didn't know anything. Who were her parents to tell her about Sunny anyway? Dawn was overcome with outrage. They knew nothing. How could it be that her parents never saw anything in another way? They saw only things the way they wanted to see them! Nothing else!

Tomorrow she would be sent away. The worst thing was that Sunny would once again have one less person to speak to. He was on his own. But what was worse? Having no family, or a family that doesn't understand you and let you be who you want to be? Family should be the center or everything, the center of life, the center of love. Without family we are alone—unless of course you believe in God. Even with God on your side, you can feel lost and alone. There is something unique about having a human companion. Dawn longed to have her own family and her own companion. For the last year or two, she had felt part of a family that, although she knew loved they her very much, she felt the need to be separated from them. Was it selfish, she wondered? Maybe it was just a part of growing up, she thought.

Dawn found herself lost in her own thoughts about life. As we grow up we see life in a different light, sometimes for better, and sometimes for worse. We learned to see things through our own lenses. We saw things the way we wanted to see them. Sometimes that was a better choice and sometimes not. We learned that life does not happen in black and white. Life is an ever-changing revolving door. As we grow up we learn that a whole world exists outside the bubble that our parents gave us. Then the only option we have is to make our decisions and choose whether or not we want to fly.

Chapter 6: Nowhere to Run or Hide

The events that followed the day of the smoothie were a blur to both Dawn and Sunny. Sunny went to Dawn's family's stand to find it closed. He was concerned but decided not to worry too much. For certain something had come up at home. Then again, that was also what he was worried about. What happened at home? Was it because he met her outside the market? Did someone see them together?

Sunny began panicking, but not too much, because like always, he found a solution. He knew how to handle almost every possible problem. Running he was good at. Actually, it was his specialty. So was hiding. The thing about being a former foster kid is that you learn how to run and hide. He didn't want to run this time. He finally had a job, an address, a roof over his head. Sunny passed the whole week trying not to be concerned when the stand didn't open. Finally, a week later the stand opened again, but still Dawn was nowhere to be found. A woman, probably Dawn's mother, was operating their fruit and vegetable stand. He knew that asking her where Dawn was could make things worse for Dawn so he simply passed the stand slowly looking for any sign that Dawn had been there or was okay.

As he passed the woman at the stand studied him with a fierce gaze. Her eyes followed Sunny across the market and watched his every move. Very conscious of the fact that he was being watched, he ducked out of the market and cut down an alley in the opposite direction of his apartment. If this was life, he wasn't sure why he existed. Perhaps worse than being orphaned was the knowledge that his mother had been pregnant when his parents died in the car crash. He never knew what it was like to have a sister or brother, but guessed that if he had been left with a brother or sister, at least they could have been there for each other.

Meanwhile Dawn woke up on the far side of the Pennsylvania border. The sun rose over Tennessee on her Uncle Kemp's property. Uncle Kemp was a quiet stern man with rules, a wood-burning stove, and a dog. Uncle Kemp never married and most of the family thought he was slightly strange. Dawn's uncle left the Amish years ago and was rarely in contact with his family. He left the community not because he minded the simple life, but actually, because he'd had a relationship with an English girl and was banished from the house. After the relationship ended, he didn't want to be with anyone else, quite literally. He took the failed union as a sign that he was to live alone.

Nobody even knew what he did to make a living and nobody asked either. Dawn found some small comfort in her Uncle's cooking and the dog, a Yorkshire Collie with thick white and black fur. She loved nothing more than to cuddle up to him, especially when she needed to cry, which was more often than not these days. She helped her Uncle Kemp in all but silence as she learned to cut wood for the fire, maintain the property, and prepare meals for the two of them.

Her parents must have thought that sending her away to her Uncle's would make her beg to come home. Dawn was not going to beg to come home. That was not part of her plan. She would stay here as long as they made her stay. She didn't care about anything. Well, almost anything. There was the issue of Sunny. She found herself thinking about where Sunny was or if Sunny thought she left the market to avoid him, or perhaps he thought that she didn't like him. Actually, the opposite was true. She was realizing that she did like him, more than she thought she did.

Chapter 7: Connections

The difficult part of finding a missing person is that either the person does not want to be found, or is being held against their will. There were few to no clues about the whereabouts of Dawn. Due to Sunny's long history of learning how to survive, hide, and get needed information, Sunny knew that if he was patient, eventually he would find out where Dawn had disappeared to. He lurked around the market listening for any information about her whereabouts. Most of the sellers at Amish community stands were tight lipped. If they knew something, they weren't telling. Many of the regulars didn't know anything about Dawn, but sellers at neighboring stands, with whom Dawn was friendly, surely did. About two weeks had passed before Sunny had a stroke of luck. He was standing in the line of shops behind the row where Dawn's family's store was located. He overhead a conversation that he had been waiting to hear.

"...too bad about Dawn, really. She is a nice girl," said the one candle shop owner.

"I always thought those Amish people were a bit strange," replied the lady who owned the pastry stand.

"You know, I heard they took her away entirely. To Tennessee, I think. Yeah, the mother said to me that she was going to her Uncle Kemp's place to stay awhile. Who knows how long she'll be gone," answered the candle shop owner.

"If I didn't know any better, I would have thought those two were together anyway. Maybe they were an item, you know," said the pastry stand owner.

"Anyway, it's better to keep your eyes to your own business," stated the candle shop owner.

That was all Sunny needed to hear. They took her out of state to Tennessee to an Uncle Kemp's house. Not as much information as he would have liked, but it was certainly a good start. It had been two weeks already since he last saw Dawn and he wasn't going to let the smoothie date be the last one.

Sunny informed his employer he was going on a personal business trip and hoped that he would still have his job and his apartment when he returned. He just paid the rent again so for now he would be okay.

Sunny left the next morning before dawn broke. He paused thinking about how lovely dawn was and how perfectly named his friend Dawn was. He would find her. With a one-way bus ticket to

Nashville, Tennessee, a granola bar, a water bottle, a change of clothes, an extra pair of boxers, a smartphone and charger, a half-full small notebook with a pen in the spiral binding, and a paper map of Tennessee in his backpack, Sunny boarded the Greyhound. Sunny knew Greyhound buses very well. More than once he'd had to utilize a fake ID to buy a Greyhound ticket to escape a foster family. Although Sunny mused it was probably unnecessary to find Dawn as she wasn't in any real peril, he felt somewhat obligated in that it was very likely his fault they took her away.

More importantly, he'd never felt like he could actually be with anyone before, the way he felt about Dawn. Despite all his jokes and flirting, he did truly have feelings for her. The bus to Nashville took a good sixteen hours. It could have been done in a lot less time, but the bus stopped in every little town known to man. How was it possible? Every hour that passed Sunny found himself getting more anxious, a feeling which was new to him. He was used to feeling in control, even when he was completely alone.

Upon arriving in Nashville, he appreciated the reality that Dawn could still be anywhere within the state. He only had the name "Uncle Kemp" to go on. Sunny found a café with a free Wi-Fi sign, ordered a grilled ham and cheese sandwich and a coke and politely asked for the password. The waitress gave him the password and quickly walked away. For certain he smelled like Greyhound bus. That was never a good smell. He always met the strangest people with unique stories on Greyhound buses, but this time, he wasn't interested in chatting with anyone.

A few minutes later, Sunny's grilled ham and cheese arrived with his coke, a pile of Lay's potato chips, and a dill pickle. After immediately devouring the sandwich, chips, and pickles, he opened his smartphone and typed in cities in Tennessee. He made a list of the largest cities of Tennessee and did a person search for the name "Kemp." There were only 13 Kemps listed in Tennessee and one of them must be the uncle.

One by one he found phone number for 11 of the 13 Kemps. He hoped that Dawn's Uncle Kemp was not one of the 2 Kemps that didn't have a phone number.

One by one he crossed off Kemps from the list. One number belonged to a woodworking business, another to a dentist's office, another three were disconnected, and a sixth and seventh number appeared to be retirees. Sunny was feeling all but completely discouraged as he made it to the 11th number. When he dialed it, a man answered the phone and said, "Hello, Kemp here." Sunny hung up immediately. The area code proved to be in Gatlinburg. Gatlinburg it was, then. Sunny rented a room for the night, got some rest, and started off early the next morning for Gatlinburg. Another Greyhound and then a few local buses later, Sunny stepped off into Gatlinburg.

Chapter 8: Fate

While Sunny was searching the town for Dawn's uncle, Dawn herself was in despair. When would she see Sunny again? Could she return to the market? What about her dream of becoming a nurse? Was her family ever going to come back for her? Reality started to sink in that maybe her mother and father were not coming back for her. She was trapped in Gatlinburg, Tennessee. As Dawn began to panic, Sunny grew closer to finding her.

As fate would have it, finally in a local McDonald's a cashier knew the name Kemp and told him where the man lived. The worker told Sunny "Yeah, he's just a few miles away. I live in that direction and I can drop you off on the right road when my shift is over." "Thanks, that would be great. Name's Sunny, by the way," said Sunny. Two hours later Sunny was sitting in a stranger's car and growing closer to his destination.

Dawn was outside in the woods preparing a fire for the evening as the sun began to set. Her Uncle was inside, quiet as usual, preparing some sausages for the fire, when Sunny rounded the bend in the road. Dawn was startled as she recognized him, screamed, and jumped up.

Her Uncle came running, and found an equal surprise in recognizing what was transpiring. Sunny, the boy that his sister wanted to keep away from his niece, has somehow tracked her down to this unlikely location. Well, since the boy was here already, there was no sense in throwing him back into the street at night. They would of course have separate rooms on opposite sides of the house.

The three found themselves face to face in front of the fire. Uncle Kemp approached Sunny before Dawn did. "So, you must be Sunny," said Uncle Kemp. "Yessir," replied Sunny. Uncle Kemp started slowly "Well, as you can see, I'm not too keen on visitors, but since you're already here, you may as well have a sausage or two."

Dawn carefully and awkwardly wandered over to Sunny as they embraced fully—not to mention quickly, as not to upset their host and make him uncomfortable. "I assume you two understand I take no responsibility for Sunny being here. And he will not sleep in the same room as you. Meanwhile, I should notify your parents that he's here, but I don't think that will be necessary," stated Uncle Kemp.

Uncle Kemp bowed his head and went inside to give them a few moments of privacy. "How did you find me?" asked Dawn. "I'm an ex-foster kid, remember. I know how to find anyone and how to lose anyone," replied Sunny. "Right, of course," said Dawn. "Look, I don't know what to say. I like you a lot. And I don't know how I feel about being stuck here in Tennessee," continued Dawn. Sunny replied, "Well, it sounds like a pretty awful thing, but your folks do care about you, I'm sure. They just care about you in a way that doesn't make sense for you."

Dawn leaned her head on Sunny's shoulder. His body was warm, his voice was endearing, but he very much needed a shower. "Um, Sunny, let's talk after you bathe. What do you think?" asked Dawn. "Haha, of course," replied Sunny. He chuckled as Dawn asked her Uncle if Sunny could shower. While Sunny cleaned himself, Uncle

Kemp left a clean pair of jeans and a plaid button-down shirt on the sink for him to wear.

To Uncle Kemp, Sunny seemed all right. Dawn and Sunny reminded him of when he was a kid. Kids want to be able to experiment in relationships. It's hard in today's world to keep an Amish kid within the confines of being Amish. After Sunny rejoined the fire the three sat together, lost in their thoughts. What they would do? Sunny and Dawn may care for each other a lot, but they had quite the decision to make, and soon. Uncle Kemp reluctantly told them his story about how he ended up living on his own. He told them about the English girl he fell in love with when he was 18. He told them it was their decision to make.

The fire dimmed and no logs were added to the dying embers. The night was not their friend, explained Uncle Kemp. He didn't believe in staying outside without the fire. The night belongs to evil. "We go inside," he said. Uncle Kemp showed Sunny where he could sleep.

Chapter 9: Dawn

Dawn arrived in a peculiar way. The sun rose quietly, the sky lit up with yellows, blue and even a little bit of orange. When the morning came, it seemed like there was no easy decision to make. There wasn't. Dawn could try to reconnect with her family, or she could stay and start over with Sunny. It was evident that Uncle Kemp was not going to stop them from making their own decision.

"Good morning, Dawn!" chanted Sunny. Sunny started singing and dancing circles around Dawn. As she laughed he pulled her into his arms and kissed her lightly on the lips. "Would you like to come with me? We can go anywhere we want," said Sunny with great optimism.

"I don't know, Sunny. We hardly know each other. You're a good boy, a good man, but I think we both have decisions to make." Dawn was trying to be even-handed and rational. Sunny tried to meet her halfway. "Let's do this, then. Let's go home. Ask your parents' permission to date me. We'll tell them everything. If they accept, that's great. If they don't, you have to decide what life you want for yourself, Dawn. Don't let them hold you back from anything. Be who you are," implored Sunny.

By 10am the two were packed and ready to leave with Uncle Kemp's blessing. He dropped them both at the highway with their backpacks and wished them the best. Since he was a man of few words, his last sentence was only one: "Godspeed."

Dawn and Sunny both nodded and found their way back to the center of Galinburg. Soon they were at the Greyhound station once more. A few hot dogs from a food truck proved to be enough to fill their stomachs as they made their way to Nashville. In Nashville, they decided to press forward through the night on an overnight bus. The whole way Dawn and Sunny found themselves engaged in pleasant conversation. Sunny admitted that he had a gun, but it was only to defend himself. Dawn needed no more explanations, only peace, time, and patience. She fell asleep in his arms on the bus as it rolled along through the night.

They washed themselves at Sunny's house in the morning and planned to go to her parents' house the next morning at dawn, for which she was well named. Dawn knocked on the door with Sunny next to her side. The door opened and she said, "Hi Mom. This is Sunny. He is my boyfriend. If you can accept us both, we'd like to come inside."